SHADOW
WALKERS

BRENT
HARTINGER

SHADOW WALKERS

Woodbury, Minnesota

First Edition
First Printing, 2011

Cover design by Kevin R. Brown
Cover images © 2010
      Lighthouse: iStockphoto.com/Vladimir Piskunov
      Boy: iStockphoto.com/Juanmonino
      Sky: iStockphoto.com/Jean-Louis Bouzou
      Nebula: iStockphoto.com/Antti-Pekka Lehtinen
      Clock: C. Anderson/Brand X Pictures

Flux, an imprint of Llewellyn Worldwide Ltd.

Library of Congress Cataloging-in-Publication Data
Hartinger, Brent.
  Shadow walkers : Brent Hartinger.
    p. cm.
  Summary: Living with his grandparents on a tiny island off the Washington coast, Zach feels cut off from the world, but when his little brother, Gilbert, is kidnapped, Zach and a new friend, Emory, seek him in the astral realm, where a centuries-old creature hungers for Zach's soul.
  ISBN 978-0-7387-2364-8
  [1. Supernatural—Fiction. 2. Astral projection—Fiction. 3. Kidnapping—Fiction. 4. Brothers—Fiction. 5. Orphans—Fiction. 6. Homosexuality—Fiction. 7. Washington (State)—Fiction.] I. Title.
  PZ7.H2635Sh 2011
  [Fic]—dc22

                      2010037547

Flux
Llewellyn Worldwide Ltd.
2143 Wooddale Drive
Woodbury, MN 55125-2989
www.fluxnow.com

Printed in the United States of America

For Michael
My own defense against the darkness

1

I felt this weird chill, so cold it made me gasp.

After first I thought I'd walked through a pocket of frozen air, but it didn't feel cold exactly, at least not on my skin. It was a much deeper chill, like I was suddenly cold on the inside of my body.

It felt like a premonition of something terrible.

But as soon as I felt it, it was gone. I'd barely had time to shiver.

I turned and looked behind me on the trail, but didn't see anything unusual. I'd been walking to the end of Trumble Point, this little peninsula at the southern tip of Hinder Island. The waters of Puget Sound in Washington State—sparkling blue and mostly calm today—stretched out on either side of me. The whole peninsula was a park, a mix of Douglas-fir and red-barked Madrona trees, but at the moment I'd felt the chill, I'd been in a clearing of bright sunlight.

I thought about taking a couple of steps back on the trail, to see if I could find the pocket of cold air again. But the truth is the chill had me spooked. I didn't *want* to feel it again, not even by reaching out with just my hand.

"Zach, come *on*!"

It was my seven-year-old brother Gilbert calling to me from farther up the trail. We'd come here together to walk to the old lighthouse at the tip of the point. It was an old-fashioned lighthouse, built high atop the rocky edge just above the beach. You couldn't go inside—it had been fully automated for years—but to the state's credit, they still kept it lit because of the row of nasty rocks that extended out from the point, invisible at high tide. The lighthouse made a great destination for a hike, especially on a beautiful summer day in June with the air smelling of pine needles and salt.

"I'm coming, I'm coming," I said, more than happy to leave the strange chill behind.

Gilbert and I had lived with our grandparents on Hinder Island for almost two years now, ever since our parents had been killed when the barrier at a railroad crossing had malfunctioned. There were only about 4,000 people on the whole island, so it was mostly just mossy forests and rocky beaches slathered with seaweed. Our grandparents had lived here forever, even raised a family, including my dad. But they were old now and didn't get off the island much. As a result, Gilbert and I didn't leave much either.

He came running back toward me, unstoppable in squeaky new tennis shoes. He was chowing down on a king-size 3 Musketeers.

"There's a dead bird in the woods!" he said. "It's grey and furry, but I think it's a baby bald eagle."

"Hold on," I said. "Where'd you get candy?"

He was suddenly wary, protective of his candy bar. "The lady."

"What lady?" I said, looking around. I hadn't seen anyone in the park so far, but that wasn't surprising. Lots of people took the ferry out to Hinder Island on the weekends, shopping in its funky art galleries and holing up in all the bed-and-breakfasts. But almost no one stayed through the week, even in summer.

"The lady with the big purse," he said, even as he kept wolfing down the chocolate in case I might try to take it from him.

"Gilbert! You know you're not supposed to take candy from strangers."

"She's not a stranger," he said, talking with his mouth full. He thought for a second. "I just don't know her name."

So she was an islander. That was different. It was true there were no "strangers" on Hinder Island. This is hard to explain to off-islanders, but things are different when you live on a small piece of land surrounded by water on all sides. After a while, you start to think of the water like a moat, like you're protected from all the bad things that happen everywhere else, safe from the Big Bad Wolf. Plus, you really *do* know all the people. It isn't long before there isn't anyone you haven't talked to at least once. And even if you've only talked to them a few times, you soon know who they know, what they do, where they live—and somehow that makes everyone accountable to everyone else.

Even so, I wasn't about to let Gilbert eat that candy. I held out my hand. "How about I hold that until we get home?"

With a heavy sigh that sounded like he was the disapproving older brother, Gilbert handed me the candy, although there was only a bite or two left. I wrapped it up as best I could—it was melting in the sun—and put it in my pocket.

"Hey, a walking stick!" Gilbert said, picking a branch up out of the undergrowth. It was almost perfectly straight and just his size. He started peeling off the leaves and smaller branches. Now that the candy bar was out of his sight, he'd forgotten all about it. Seven-year-olds.

"Wanna hear something interesting?" Gilbert said as we started forward again, him with the walking stick.

"Sure," I said.

"Billy says he stuck a branch in the swamp, and two weeks later, it started to grow leaves. It turned into a tree!"

"That *is* interesting."

"You think that works with people too? If I cut off my arm and stuck it in the swamp, I'd grow a whole new me?"

I stopped on the trail. "No. Gilbert, it doesn't work that way with people. You know that, right?"

He turned around to face me, leaning against his stick. "Yeah. I just wanted to know what you'd say."

I rolled my eyes at him.

When we'd started walking again, he said, "You wanna know something else interesting?"

"Sure," I said.

"You think I'm gonna forget about my candy bar in your pocket. But I won't."

Leave it to my little brother to be anything but a typical seven-year-old.

"You little Nabothian cyst!" I said, using my pet nickname for him. A year or so earlier, he overheard our grandparents saying that our mother had once had one of these, which are these harmless little bumps inside a woman's body. Gilbert had asked me what it was, and I'd impulsively said that it was him, that *he* was a Nabothian cyst. Gilbert hadn't believed me, but I'd said, "You know how Grandma is always saying Mom 'had' you? 'When Cecil *had* Gilbert ...'? Well, that's what she means. Mom *had* a Nabothian cyst. You!"

I'd been teasing him about it ever since. For some reason, it felt really good to laugh about something that involved our parents.

"I am not!" Gilbert said.

"Are too," I said, pretending to be serious. "I don't know why you still don't believe me."

He squealed with laughter. We'd been playing this game a long time, but for some reason it wasn't making me feel very good today. I'd been wrong when I'd thought I could leave that chill in the air behind—that pocket of cold air or whatever it was—just by walking on down the trail. I still couldn't shake the sense that something terrible was going to happen.

"There's the lighthouse!" Gilbert said, pointing.

Sure enough, it loomed up from a rocky crag at the very end of the trail.

In front of us, the trail split in three ways—a narrow access trail heading up to the lighthouse, and two wider trials that wound their way down to the rocky beaches on either side of the point.

Out in the water, seagulls circled and crab-trap buoys rocked.

I hated that water. Those same waterways that kept bad things away, that kept everything safe and predictable, also kept out new faces and new ideas. It's not like the women on Hinder Island wore bonnets on their heads and accused people of being witches like in that play *The Crucible*. But it was like living in a small town: everyone was just a little too literal in their thinking, and a little too suspicious of outsiders. And while everyone knew everyone else, everyone also knew everyone else's business. This is all fine when you're seven like Gilbert or in your seventies like my grandparents. It's not so great when you're sixteen and the new kid in town, like I had been for—well, two whole years now.

Once you set foot on an island, no matter which direction you go, sooner or later you come to a dead end.

Something caught my eye down on the beach on my right.

It was Matt Harken, this guy a couple of years ahead of me in school. He'd climbed up on one of the beach's big boulders and was fishing—alone, it looked like. This made sense. He was a loner, but definitely not a loser—like how I'd like to think people saw me, even if I was probably just flattering myself. Matt was sort of a cross between a geek and hipster, neither cool enough to be noticed nor weird enough to be mocked. And he almost never *was* noticed, not by most people.

I'd noticed him. I guess you could say I had kind of a crush on him.

But I'd never even talked to him. I take back what I said about how I'd talked to every single person on the island at least once. I'd never had the nerve to talk to Matt.

It's funny how you could know by sight every single person on an island of 4,000 people and still not have a single real friend, much less anything "more."

Matt wasn't wearing a shirt, just shorts.

I'd always thought he was a good-looking guy, but it was kind of a hidden beauty, which I guess is why more people didn't see it. He had a rare, confident smile. And his longish dark hair hung down over eyes that were so piercing they were like whaling harpoons.

But I had never seen his shirtless body before. His back bulged. He was pale, but not pasty, lean, but not skinny. Casting his rod, he turned in silhouette, and I saw his chest and stomach was rippled in all the right places. He had the same dusting of dark hair on his chest that he had on his legs—legs that looked particularly muscled as he stood perched on that granite boulder.

For the first time since that weird chill, I felt myself flush warm again. I knew I should look away, keep walking after Gilbert, but I couldn't tear my eyes away. I was in the shadows of the trees, and he was out in the sun of the beach—even if he did know I was there, I doubted he'd be able to see me.

But just then the sun dipped behind some clouds, and he must've somehow sensed me ogling him. Anyway, he turned around to look right up at me. This figured.

I immediately looked away. How embarrassing. I wondered how obvious it had been that I'd been staring.

I hurried forward, not daring to look back. Face flushed, I reminded myself that I really needed to keep an eye on Gilbert, especially this close to the water.

"Gilbert?" I said, but he didn't answer. "Gilbert?" I said, louder.

I'd seen him go down the left-hand trail, but I couldn't see him ahead of me. This made me mad. He knew he wasn't supposed to go all the way down to the beach alone.

"Gilbert!" I said, working my way down the grade to the beach itself. It was steeper than I remembered, and a skittering of loose rocks following behind me like a little avalanche.

At the bottom of the trail, Gilbert's walking stick had been tossed to one side. Not stuck in the sand, not resting against a tree.

The granite boulders on the beach were taller on this side of the point, almost over my head. They loomed up like tombstones in some giant graveyard.

"Gilbert!" I said. "Where *are* you?"

There was still no answer.

I remembered that chill I'd felt, that premonition I'd had. I'd *known* something bad was going to happen—and I'd still allowed myself to be distracted by Matt. How could I have been so stupid?

"*Gilbert!*" I yelled, suddenly frantic. The waves weren't exactly crashing against the shore—there are no crashing waves in the protected waters of Puget Sound. But the slopping of the water against the beach was just loud enough that I couldn't be sure how far my voice would carry, especially within all those boulders.

Still calling for him, I started searching between the rocks. I'd been here dozens of times before, but it had never felt so much like a maze. My feet crunched in the wet, dark gravel. Overhead, clouds claimed more of the sky. I didn't know how they'd moved in that quickly.

"*Gilbert!*" I yelled. I thought about calling for Matt, but I was sure he couldn't hear me, not completely on the other side of the point. I even looked around for the woman who had given Gilbert that candy, hoping that she might be able to help me.

I stepped behind one giant rock, then another, then another. The waves splashing against the beach seemed bigger now—a fishing boat must've passed by just offshore, but I hadn't seen or heard it go by.

I was in a full-fledged panic now. I remembered the chill, the certainty that something terrible was about to occur, and it made me gasp all over again.

I stepped behind one more boulder.

And there was Gilbert, sitting on his haunches staring into a tidal pool. The tide pool itself was completely still even as a wave crashed against a rock not five feet away.

He barely looked up at me. "There's a crab with only one claw," he said.

I was so relieved I couldn't bring myself to speak, much less yell at him. Instead, I turned toward the open water, looking out at the darkening sky.

A cold breeze suddenly blew in off the bay, but I didn't shiver. Whatever had caused the chill I'd felt before, it had been a lot colder than this.

2

The first thing that strikes you about being on an island like Hinder is the sounds. There are a lot fewer of them, so you notice more of the ones you hear.

As Gilbert and I rode our bikes back home from Trumble Point, I couldn't help but listen to the sounds of the island.

Unseen squirrels chirped in the woods.

A breeze rustled through the leaves of the trees.

A horn blasted from an approaching ferry.

I could never figure out why the sound of the ferry carried the way it did. The landing was way at the north end of the island. As a result, that's where most of the people lived. But Gilbert and I lived with our grandparents in an old farmhouse toward the south end of the island, a ten-minute bike ride from Trumble Point. The whole area had once been an apple orchard. Most of it had been reclaimed by forest, but many of the old apple trees lived on, their trunks getting knottier, their unpruned branches growing ever more wild. Some of them still grew apples in the fall, but they were now too small and too sour to eat.

I still hadn't forgotten that strange chill I'd felt back at the point—or the scare I'd had when I'd thought Gilbert was missing. But the closer we got to home, the more that all seemed like a distant memory.

A dock creaked down along the water beyond the trees.

A hummingbird buzzed by right in front of my bike.

And angry voices rose up from the front porch of the house across the street from our grandparents.

"Margaret!" one voice said, a man. "Be reasonable. Do you have any idea how much that thing cost?"

"So buy him a new one!" another voice said, a woman. "If he wants to keep it here, he's keeping it here, and that's final."

"At this point, I've lost track of how many ways you're violating the terms of our custody agreement!"

"You're one to talk about violating agreements."

You could count the houses of our neighbors on one hand. These voices were coming from the house of Gilbert's best friend, a six-year-old boy named Billy who lived there with his mother. His parents were divorced, and his father didn't live on the island anymore. But due to some weird wording on the custody agreement, the mother had worked it so that if the father wanted to see his son, he had to take the ferry all the way out to the island to pick Billy up at her house, then later bring him all the way back home again.

For this and many other reasons, they now hated each other with a passion—and that hatred often dissolved into screaming matches on the front porch of the house.

Like I said, everyone on the island knew everyone else's business, including me.

———

At least I had the Internet.

If an island was a place of endless dead ends, the Internet was the exact opposite: a world without limits. You could go anywhere at any time. Better still, you could do it from the comfort of your own bedroom.

The first thing I did when I got home, even before I took off my shoes, was to go up to my bedroom so I could update my profile status. I'd have done it out at Trumble Point with my phone, but there wasn't any service that far south.

I thought about writing about that weird chill I'd felt, that premonition or whatever. But a bigger part of me was determined to forget all about it. Besides, I could never write it in such a way that people would truly understand.

I also thought about writing what had happened to Gilbert, but I didn't particularly want to be reminded about that either.

Gilbert and I just got back from the beach, I wrote. *Wounded Wolf was there fishing. Shirtless. OMFG.*

Wounded Wolf was the nickname I'd given Matt. I wasn't about to call him by his real name, not where someone on the island might see. The first time I'd mentioned him, I'd said he reminded me of a wolf caught in a trap, and the name had just kind of stuck. Plus, there was that whole piercing-brown-eyes thing.

Then I started uploading a video Gilbert and I had taken of some centipedes scurrying around under this rotten stump. Most of the people I knew online lived in the city, so I figured if I was forced to live on Hinder Island, I could at least share a little bit of nature with them. It was just one of my "things."

By the time the video was uploaded, the comments started coming in fast and furious about my profile update.

Photos! Kelsey commented. *We wanna see Wounded Wolf shirtless!*

LOL, I wrote. *Didn't take any. I may be a perv, but not that much of one.*

A text box popped up in my window.

Details! Smuggler16 wrote. *We want details!*

I laughed out loud for real this time.

I take back what I said about not having any friends. Maybe I didn't have any on Hinder Island, but that didn't mean I didn't have any friends at all. They were just the online kind. True, I'd never met any of them in person, but I'd known a couple of them since before my parents died.

These were people who accepted me the way I was, including the whole gay thing. My grandparents weren't Neanderthals, but they were in their seventies, and that was a conversation I just did not want to be having with them any time soon. And the rest of Hinder Island? Please. The island was only a couple of miles from the mainland, from the south end of Tacoma, with Seattle thirty miles to the north. But it might as well have been a whole ocean.

Sometimes it was like the life I lived online was the real one, and my life on Hinder Island, that was the fake one.

I started filling in the requested details about Matt's body—I still hadn't gotten a chance to upload some photos I'd taken of a starfish eating a clam—when there was a knock on my door.

"Come in," I said.

It was my grandparents. Together. That was a little weird. But even so, I barely glanced over at them.

"Zach?" my grandpa said.

"We need to talk to you," my grandma said.

"Go for it," I said.

"We need to you to stop typing," my grandpa said.

"And give us your full attention," my grandma said.

My grandparents said this a lot. They hated how much time I spent on the computer. They were always saying how there were all these bad people online.

"There's so much evil in the world," my grandmother would say. "Why would you want to bring that into your bedroom?"

My grandfather would always agree. "That's why we live here on Hinder," he'd say. "So we don't have to worry about that kind of stuff."

When it came to anything off-island, my grandparents had always been the nervous types, but ever since my parents had been killed, they'd been more paranoid than ever. It had been over a year since I'd bothered arguing with them about any of this.

I stopped typing. I didn't want my grandparents seeing anything suspicious on my profile, so I turned off the monitor. Then I turned and gave them my full attention.

As grandparents go, mine were okay. I'm sure they hadn't expected to be raising kids again, not in their seventies. Still, they were fit and active. After a lifetime of being together, they'd even started to look like each other. They now had just about the same amount of thinning white hair. And over the years, my grandma had put on some pounds and my grandpa had lost a few inches of height, so they were now both almost the same size. If you didn't know any better, you might think they were twins—maybe even twins of the same sex.

Just like twins, they also had this habit of finishing each other's sentences.

"It's Thursday, Zachary," my grandpa said.

"Garbage day," my grandma said.

I forgot to take the garbage out, I thought. We had to keep the garbage in the garage because of raccoons, and on garbage day, it was my job to haul it down to the curb for the collectors. Today had been garbage day, but Gilbert and I had left for Trumble Point on our bikes before I'd gotten around to it.

"We don't ask you to do a lot around here," my grandma said.

"But it's really important that you do that," my grandpa said.

"Because you didn't do it today, your grandfather had to," my grandma said. "And it's far too heavy for him, and he fell down and skinned his knee."

"Mary, I'm fine," my grandpa said.

"That's not the point!" my grandma said.

"I'm really sorry," I said. "I totally forgot. Gilbert and I rode our bikes out to—"

"It seems like you forget a lot," my grandpa said.

"Not that much," I said.

"We're at our wits' end trying to get you to remember," my grandma said.

"But we think you might be more likely to if you're punished," my grandpa said.

"As of tonight, we want you off your computer for one week," my grandma said.

It took a second for the words to sink in. No computer? For a whole week? They couldn't be serious.

"And your phone too," my grandpa said. "If you need to make a call, you can use the line in the house."

"But—" How did I explain to them what a big deal this was to me? Without the computer, without contact with my friends, being on Hinder Island would be like being in prison.

"It's just as well," my grandma said. "It's just not right, how you're always on that thing. It's going to lead to something bad, I just know it."

That's when I knew there was nothing I could say to change their minds. They'd been looking for an excuse to take my computer away anyway.

"And if this kind of thing ever happens again," my grandpa said, "we'll take your phone and your computer away for good."

————

But just because my grandparents had made up their minds, that didn't mean I wasn't going to *try* to change them. Of course no matter how I tried to talk them into a different punishment, they wouldn't listen. All my arguing was just proof that they'd stumbled upon a punishment that might really have an impact on me.

After a while, even Gilbert pulled me aside. "Zach?" he said to me, with all the maturity of his seven years. "Give it up. You're just making it worse."

To make things even more dire, we didn't have a television—it had been hard enough talking them into getting me an Internet connection. I'd never really cared that we didn't have TV because I watched everything online or on my phone, but what was I going to do now for the next week?

"Why don't we all play a game of hearts?" my grandma said after dinner.

The offline world can't be that *boring*, I thought.

On Hinder Island, it could.

"I'm going up to my room," I said, which is exactly what I did.

But once I got there, I realized there wasn't anything more interesting there either, not with my computer out. My bedroom had been my dad's when he was a kid, and it hadn't really changed since then. It had the same saggy bed he'd slept in, with a couple of torn STP stickers stuck to the headboard. There was a matching nightstand and dresser, but a different desk, much older with darker wood, some kind of antique. And he'd tacked a poster from the 1980s movie *Poltergeist* to the wall, though it was now pretty faded.

It was funny. I'd never really noticed how little I'd changed the room since moving in with my grandparents two years earlier. Partly it was the fact that I spent most of my life online, so I didn't really care what my room looked like. But it was also the way Gilbert and I had ended up here after our parents had been killed. My grandparents had never really talked about it, never officially said to us, "We're going to raise you now. This is your new home." As a result, it had always kind of felt like I was living in one of their spare bedrooms. I'd never really thought about it before, but maybe this was part of the reason why I spent so much time online.

I paced around my bedroom for a while until I was almost desperate enough to go back and join my grandparents for that game of hearts, but then I heard the creaking of old pipes and squeaking of old floorboards as my grandpa started getting a bath ready for Gilbert.

Shortly after that, my grandparents got themselves ready for bed, too. A few minutes later, the squeaks and creaks stopped. It wasn't even nine o'clock at night, and the rest of the house had already gone to bed. Did they do this every night? I'd never noticed.

And I still didn't have anything to do except lay in bed and stare at the ceiling. There sure were a lot of dead bugs in the light fixture.

My grandparents said there was all this evil in the world—out in cyberspace and out across the water that surrounded our little island.

I suddenly remembered that strange chill I'd felt out at Trumble Point.

I didn't want to think about that.

On the shelf in the bottom half of the nightstand, I spotted some books. They must've also been my dad's— another thing I'd never noticed in the two years I'd been living here.

I looked at some of the titles. *Brideshead Revisited* by Evelyn Waugh. *The Power and the Glory* by Graham Greene. Something called *Onions in the Stew* by Betty MacDonald.

No, thanks, I thought. It's not that I never read books, but I couldn't remember the last time I read them in actual book form—and I had no interest in reading anything that old.

I came to a book with the title *Voyage Beyond the Rainbow* by someone named Celestia Moonglow.

That made me sit up.

I pulled the book off the shelf. The subtitle was *The Art of Astral Projection.* From the font, it looked like it had been published in the 1970s. The cover had a picture of a man sitting in a chair with his head down. The way he was clenching the arm rests, it almost looked like he was strapped to the chair. Rising up from out of the man's body was this glowing image of the same man, arms outstretched toward the sky, this peaceful expression on his face.

I flipped the book over.

At last it can be revealed—the ancient secrets of astral travel! read the bold print at the top of the page. *Free your soul from its physical confines and send it soaring into strange new realms!*

I'd heard of astral projection. Out-of-body travel.

The writing continued in smaller type. *"For centuries, people have reported the ability to separate their souls from their bodies. Now you can try astral projection too! Author Celestia Moonglow presents the first practical, step-by-step guide to out-of-body travel. In easy-to-follow language, Celestia lays out a simple, time-tested strategy for astral projection. At last it's possible to separate your astral body from your physical one—to travel through space and time, visit distant planets, and even travel to different dimensions!*

This was crazy. Astral projection was like angel-readings and past-life regression and tarot cards and the rest of the New Age nonsense.

I put the book back on the shelf and sat back to stare up at the ceiling. I also had cobwebs in my corners.

On the other hand, the alternative to the book was staring up at my ceiling all night.

I reached for book again, opened it, and sat back on my bed and started reading.

3

By eleven o'clock, I'd finished reading *Voyage Beyond the Rainbow*. It really was a step-by-step guide to this thing called astral projection. Supposedly you could separate your soul from your body and go soaring around something called the astral realm.

The astral realm is a shadow dimension that exists alongside the material world, the book said. *People in the material dimension cannot see into the astral dimension and are usually unaware that it even exists. But occupants of the astral dimension can see things in both the astral realm and in the* material one. Still, the astral realm is a spiritual dimension, not a physical one. Nothing exists there except spirits. Even distances don't exist in the way that they do in the material world.

The way you traveled to this realm was to become so relaxed that your mind and body literally drifted apart.

It's a form of dreaming, Celestia Moonglow said. *And it many ways, it feels very much like dreaming. But it's not a dream, because you'll be in control. And unlike a dream, this is very real.*

This was all garbage, of course. An astral realm? Please. Still, I'd spent all that time reading the book, and I wasn't ready to go to bed yet. I figured I might as well give it a try. I knew it wouldn't work—but what if it did? It was a way off this stupid island that didn't involve paying for the ferry— or getting permission from my grandparents.

Astral separation only occurs when a person is very relaxed, the book said.

So I lit a candle and put on some soft music, just like the book suggested. Then I sat back in bed, as comfortable as possible. It's funny, I thought, how you don't notice all the places where your clothes pinch and bind until you're trying to relax.

At the same time, the book went on, *you have to be fully aware of everything that's going on, which requires a state of heightened awareness. We achieve this state through medita- tion. But mediation is really just a fancy name for a sustained focusing of the mind. Many people create this same height-*

ened awareness through athletics, the playing of an instru-
ment, or even prayer.

I'd never meditated before, but it's not like I found the whole concept weird. I knew what Celestia Moonglow meant about that sense of heightened awareness that comes from being really focused on something. I'd felt it when editing a video clip or writing code for a website.

I closed my eyes and began to breathe deeply. The book gave different suggestions on how to enter a meditative trance—concentrating on chimes or a mantra that you repeat over and over in your mind. But the one I liked was simply concentrating on the point in your nostrils where the air enters and leaves your body. The goal was to *become* your breathing—to focus the mind in such a way that you didn't think about anything but the air flowing in and out of your body.

I kept breathing. The only thing that existed for me was the little exchange of air at my nostrils.

In.

And.

Out.

It was harder than it sounded, blocking out awareness of yourself and your surroundings. It didn't help that the candle was smoking and I had an itch in my right ear. Once or twice, my brain may have flashed to an image of Matt, shirtless and in shorts, on the beach earlier that day.

Imagine that with each breath, you're releasing all the stresses and cares of everyday life from your body, the book said. *Feel them flowing out of you.* That's what I was try-ing to do. And with each breath, I did feel a little more relaxed.

But how relaxed was relaxed enough? You could always be *more* relaxed. The fact that I was even thinking about these things meant that I probably wasn't relaxed enough.

So I kept breathing, and kept imagining the stress flow from my body.

Long.

Deep.

Breaths.

I wasn't sure how long I went on like this, but eventu-ally I got tired of wondering if I was relaxed enough, so I decided it was time to push on.

In order to achieve the astral separation, the book said, *imagine a little point of light on your forehead.* There had even been a little diagram.

In my mind's eye, I tried to focus on that single point. It took me a moment to get a mental handle on it.

Now very slowly move that point out from your body until it's hovering about six feet above you.

I did my best to follow these instructions, imagining that little point on my forehead slowly rising up from my body, over my head.

Now imagine your spirit floating free from your body, ris-ing to join the point of light above you.

I imagined my spirit floating free.

But I still had that itch in my right ear—I'd obviously made a mistake deciding not to scratch it—and I suddenly had that mental image of Matt again.

Concentrate, the book said. *Let yourself go.*

But I couldn't concentrate. Or, rather, I *was* concentrating, but on the itch in my ear.

This wasn't working.

I tried it again from the top—the long, deep breaths, imagining the stress flowing from my body.

It didn't work the second time either.

Astral projection wasn't real, just like I'd known it wouldn't be.

———

The next morning, I actually sat down at my computer and turned it on before I remembered the punishment my grandparents had given me. To their credit, they hadn't made me move my computer into their bedroom or anything.

Then I remembered what they'd said about taking the thing away for good if I got caught doing anything else wrong, and it was all I could do to not yank the plug right out of the wall.

When the computer was off again, I realized I had the exact same problem I'd had the night before.

What am I going to do without a computer for a whole week?

I had breakfast and even washed my dishes. That took twenty minutes.

I took a shower and got dressed. That took another twenty minutes.

I cleaned the dead bugs out of the fixture on my ceiling—and took a broom and brushed out the cobwebs in the corners too. That took about fifteen minutes.

When I was done with all that, it wasn't even ten in the morning yet. How was I going to spend the rest of my day?

My grandparents had specifically forbidden me from using my computer, but they hadn't said anything at all about *another* computer. But my options were limited on a place like Hinder Island. I didn't have any real island friends. And while there was computer access at the island's public library, they were only open a couple days a week—and not for three more days. Plus, they limited the amount of time you could be on because there were usually other people waiting.

I went out onto the front porch. My grandparents were in the garage shellacking a bureau, and Gilbert and Billy were across the street chasing grasshoppers. They were two blond streaks tearing around the yard.

"Hey, Zach!" Gilbert called to me. "Come play with us!"

Once again I was so desperate I almost considered joining them. Then I remembered the island's Internet café. It was more like a couple of ancient computers-for-hire in the back of Hole in the Wall, the town's lone coffee bar, but hey, it'd do the job.

———

The town of Hinder was located in the middle of the island. It wasn't far from our house—*nowhere* was far from anywhere else on the island. I rode my bike there and stored it in this wooden rack just outside the town center. There was no need to lock it up—no one ever locked up anything on the island, not bikes, not cars, not houses.

Hinder wasn't much: a few dozen houses surrounding a weird mix of businesses, some that catered to islanders, like the hardware and grocery stores, and some that relied mostly on the weekend tourists. You could tell which were the businesses that catered to the islanders, because they were the ones that didn't ever repaint or repair their signs, if they even bothered having a sign at all.

As I turned away from my bike, I found myself facing the open garage of one of the houses on the main road leading into town. Matt Harken—Wounded Wolf—was inside, working on some project. It looked like he was carving a canoe out of an actual log—alone, of course. I'd known he lived in that house, but I'd never actually seen him outside before.

He hadn't noticed me, but I felt myself flush red anyway. After he'd caught me ogling him on the beach out at

Trumble Point, the last thing in the world I wanted was to talk to him.

Okay, I take that back. I *did* want to talk to him. That was the whole point of the fake online name and my documenting his every move. I *desperately* wanted to talk to him.

Hadn't I always said that out of all the guys on the island, he seemed the one that I had a shot with? I mean, he was carving a canoe out of a log! If I didn't talk to him, I'd never know for sure if we had any kind of connection. It's not like I had to ask him out on a date. I just wanted to introduce myself, chat a bit, and see if there was any spark—find out if there was any chance he was like me. And since I was going to be offline for a whole week, there was no better time than now to finally do it.

Weirdly, taking the idea seriously finally made my face stop turning red. I took a deep breath.

I was going to do it. I was finally going to talk to Matt.

4

I didn't talk to Matt.

I really wanted to, but I wimped out. I couldn't even bring myself to cross the street. Instead, I walked to the Hole in the Wall Internet café and spent most of the afternoon online. By the time I was done, Matt was gone.

I went back to Hole in the Wall Internet café the following day. I was still determined to talk to him.

I chickened out again.

The next day, the third day of my banishment from my computer, I actually made it across the street before I lamed out.

On the fourth day, I thought I saw Matt glance over at me. I managed to nod, but I didn't dare look at him when I did it. I was too afraid I'd be harpooned by those eyes of his.

On the fifth day, he wasn't even there.

On the sixth day, he was back working in the garage again, but he went inside just as I set foot on his driveway.

The seventh day was the last day I'd be coming to Hole in the Wall Internet café—after that my punishment was over, and I'd be allowed to use my own computer again. True, I'd run into Matt other places on the island, but this seemed like the perfect opportunity to talk to him, one where I could plan it all out in advance.

As I road my bike into town that day, I thought about exactly what I wanted to say. I'd pretend to be walking into town again, but then I'd look over at him. I'd casually stroll over to the driveway and say, "I've been coming into town all week to work on the computer, and I couldn't help but notice what you're doing. You're really carving a canoe?" Whatever it was he said, I'd smile and say, "Wow, that's really interesting. By the way, I'm Zach. You're Matt, right? We go to school together."

I was pretty nervous as I placed my bike in the rack. But I was determined to see this through. It was just talking to him. What was the big deal?

I took another deep breath and turned around to face the garage.

He wasn't there. The garage door was open and the half-carved canoe was still inside. But Matt wasn't around.

Well, that's that, I thought. I wish I could say I was disappointed, but the truth is, I was totally relieved.

I stepped out on the sidewalk—and crashed right into Matt himself. He must've crossed the street behind me and was now walking into town. I hadn't even noticed.

"Oh!" I said. "Sorry! Geez. Sorry." I'd really collided with him. He smelled like cedar sawdust and sweat, both clean.

"S'okay, man," he said, barely even glancing at me.

He wasn't alone. He'd been walking with this girl— Leigh Walsh, someone from his class. She was pretty in a cheap, beer-on-the-beach kind of way. She smelled like something sweet, but not clean—something sticky, like taffy.

She and Matt were holding hands. That's who Matt was looking at even now.

Matt had a new girlfriend. He was so caught up in her that I'd walked right into him, and he'd barely even noticed.

But Leigh had noticed. She laughed out loud. She didn't actually say, "What a dork!" but she might as well have. It'd been a long time since I'd been this embarrassed—not since, well, the week before when Matt had caught me ogling him out at Trumble Point.

I immediately turned and headed into town. But Matt and Leigh were going into town too, so they ended up walking right behind, like the three of us were walking together.

"Ask for no foam," Leigh said to Matt. "They always give me too much foam."

They were going to Hole in the Wall too—it's not like Hinder had more than one coffee bar. But the last thing in the world I wanted now was to spend time around Matt. So much for my making small talk, for my finding out if he was like me.

I stopped at the first store I came to and immediately ducked inside.

Outside, I heard Leigh laugh. At least I didn't know for *sure* that she was laughing at me.

———

It was a New Age shop called The Crystal Unicorn. I knew this because it was one of the stores in town that had a sign. Still, I'd never been inside before. In the window to one side of me, there was a collection of stone goddesses, all different, but all very fat. The air smelled of patchouli and cat box.

I looked around. It seemed to be deserted—I didn't even see the cat. A nearly dry fountain gasped from somewhere beyond the racks of angel greeting cards.

Even now, I wasn't willing to give up on the Internet café completely, but I needed to give Matt and Leigh some time to get their coffee and go. So I worked my way deeper into the store, past a table stacked with different kinds of incense and glass cases full of colorful jewelry—the kind you'd see on an Egyptian queen or a Florida retiree. One hexagonal case held small crystal figurines—dragons, sea monsters, and, yes, a unicorn—but the light had burned out, so they all looked drab and dusty.

The back wall of the shop was covered with small mirrors with odd shapes and brightly colored wooden frames—African maybe.

A cloth curtain hung over a doorway into the back of the store, with a curtain of beads dangling down over that. Now I smelled something decidedly non-New Age—something frying in oil. I wondered if there was some kind of apartment in back.

Below the mirrors, there was a table with a basket full of handmade soaps, each in a yellow wrapper with a drawing of a crescent moon. I picked one up and smelled it.

"You're Gilbert's brother," said a voice.

I jumped, startled. It was the shopkeeper behind the counter. If she'd come from the apartment in back, I wondered why I hadn't heard the beads rattle. Maybe the cloth curtain had muffled them.

She was a large woman—a little like the stone goddesses in the front window. She had frizzy red hair in a bun, freckles, and a big blue sun dress. I'd seen her around before. I take back what I said about Matt being the only person on the island I'd never talked to. I'd never talked to this woman either.

"Yeah," I said. "I am." I wasn't surprised that she knew who Gilbert and I were. It wasn't just that everyone knew everyone else on Hinder Island. Here Gilbert and I were the Boys Who Lived With Their Grandparents Because Their Parents Were Dead.

"He's such a cute little boy," the woman said. She paused. "You like how that smells?"

"Huh?"

"The soap." She meant the one in my hand, the one I'd been smelling.

"Oh," I said. "Yeah, sure. It's nice."

"It's made with lemon, cedar, and rosemary, which all have purification powers. That means that soap doesn't just clean the body, it also cleanses the soul."

"Ah."

She smiled at me. "Too much for you, eh?"

"No," I said. "No, it's interesting." I put the soap back.

"It's okay," the woman said. "I didn't always believe in all this either."

"Well, I wanted to believe, but—"

"What?"

I glanced back at the sidewalk. It was still too soon to go back outside—I didn't want to run into Matt again. Then I thought, well, why not tell her the truth?

"Last week, I found this book on astral projection," I said. "And I tried it, but it didn't work. For me, anyway."

"How long have you been meditating?"

"What? Oh, I haven't been. I mean, I just tried it for the first time last week."

She laughed. "You'd been meditating for one day, and you're disappointed that you can't do astral projection?"

"What do you mean?"

"Astral projection is really hard. Didn't the book tell you that?"

I kind of shrugged. "Yeah. I guess it did." *To enter the astral state, most people require a daily meditation regimen of a half hour a day for at least three months*, the book had said. But I'd ignored that part.

"And even then—" she started to say.

"What?"

She fiddled with a rack of pendants. "Well, what most people think of as astral projection is just a form of dreaming. Oh, they *see* into the astral realm. Sort of. But they're not actually *there*. I think we all enter the astral realm a little bit when we're dreaming. Most folks who claim they do astral projection just do the same thing a little bit more consciously."

This was basically what Celestia Moonglow had written in that book—that astral projection was a form of dreaming. Big deal.

"You said that's how *most* people do it," I said. "So some people do it differently?"

The woman in the sun dress looked up at me and smiled. "Maybe."

"You?" I said.

"Truthfully, no. It's not my thing." She lowered her voice almost to a whisper. "But I know how it's done."

"How?"

She glanced around, as if to make sure the store was still empty. Then she bent down behind the counter. I stepped closer and saw that she was rummaging around in a big satchel on the floor, almost like a carpet bag. Finally she pulled out a bundle of incense sticks wrapped up in a plastic baggie. She pulled them out of the plastic, maybe twenty sticks in all. Unlike the incense on that table, these weren't neatly wrapped in paper or packaged in boxes, just gathered in a rubberband.

I knew it was stupid—it was just a bundle of incense sticks—but the woman's secretive nature, this whole interaction with her, was exciting somehow, something dangerous in a place where nothing dangerous ever happened.

"Try this," she said, placing the incense sticks on the counter.

I picked them up and took a whiff. I didn't recognize the smell, but it reminded me of a forest, rich and complicated.

"What is it?" I asked.

"It's a special recipe. Very difficult to get." At that exact moment, I noticed a strange under-odor to the incense, like something rotten.

"Is it legal? And safe?"

She laughed. "Completely."

"How much?" I said.

"A hundred dollars," she said.

Now I laughed. "Uh, no thanks." How had I not seen *that* coming?

"It's worth it," she said. "It really works!"

"I'm sure it does," I said, starting for the door. Matt and Leigh had to have their coffees by now, and even if they didn't, I could go in some other shop.

"Tell you what," the woman said. "How about I give you a free sample?"

"No, thanks." I really wasn't interested.

"No strings! You take it home and try it. If it works and you like it, you come back and I'll sell you more at the full price."

I stopped.

"It's free! What do you have to lose?"

She had a point.

"Here, take three sticks," she said. "I can afford to be generous, because I know you'll be back."

I took them, and I really did intend to try them.

But the thing is, that was the day my punishment came to an end. And when I got home that night, my grandma said, "It still makes me sick to think about what kind of person you might run into on that computer of yours."

And my grandpa said, "But you upheld your end of the bargain. So we'll uphold ours. You're free to use it and your phone again."

So I put those three sticks of incense in the drawer of the nightstand in my bedroom, and I forgot all about them.

5

Soon the weeks of summer turned into months, and I was still stuck on my own personal Alcatraz. Now that I knew that Wounded Wolf—Matt—was straight, I didn't even have him to fantasize about.

But at least I had my computer back.

One morning in mid-July, I tore myself away from the monitor to take the garbage out. I hate to say it, but my grandparents' punishment had worked: I hadn't forgotten to take the garbage out even a single time since then.

My grandparents were battling slugs in the garden out back, but Gilbert was on the front lawn playing with one of the neighborhood cats.

"What you doing?" I asked him.

"Playing fetch," he said. He held up a stick.

"You play fetch with a dog, not with a cat," I said.

"Oh, yeah? Watch!" He tossed the stick across the grass. The grey cat bolted after it.

Gilbert beamed.

"But he isn't bringing the stick back," I said. The cat was busy clawing at the wood. A second later, he forgot the stick completely and pounced on a nearby leaf. "See?"

"He still fetched it."

I wasn't going to argue. "Where's Billy today?"

Gilbert looked glum. "He and his mom went off-island."

"Sorry about that," I said as I turned back for the house.

As I sat at my computer, I could hear the sounds of the island through my open window.

Crows cawed.

A neighbor's wind chimes jingled in the breeze.

Gilbert squealed with laughter. If I didn't know better, I'd have thought he really had taught that cat to return the stick.

By early afternoon, I was still sitting at the computer. Outside my window, a truck rattled by, and a bell rang in the distance.

I realized I'd been inside all morning. Plus, it had been weeks since I'd taken any photos or videos of the island—supposedly my "thing." Some neighbor-friends of my grandparents had given me permission to borrow their rowboat whenever I wanted, so I decided to take it out into the bay.

My grandfather was washing dishes in the kitchen. I told him where I was going, then looked around for Gilbert. I didn't see him, so I assumed that Billy must be back and they'd run off together.

I rowed around on the water for a couple of hours. When I finally got back to shore, I felt just as trapped by the island as ever, but now my arms hurt.

———

I was almost back to my grandparents' house when I saw the silent pulse of flashing blue and red lights from the road up ahead.

The police car was parked on my grandparents' side of the street. The siren was off, but I could hear the clicks of its flashing lights even from 100 yards away. There was a sheriff's car parked just beyond it.

I felt a vague, but familiar, chill.

I started walking faster. There are no sidewalks on most of the island, and suddenly I was aware of all the gravel and tree debris that had collected on the shoulder of the road.

Up ahead, I could hear the low rumble of male voices and an old woman's whimper.

Was something wrong with Grandpa? But there wasn't an ambulance. Besides, they would've called me. Then I remembered I'd been out on the water where there wasn't any cell phone service.

I started running. My feet kicked at the gravel and tree branches. One of the neighbors had just cut their lawn, and the smell of cut grass filled my nostrils.

As I got closer, I noticed something I'd missed in the flashing of the police car lights: a little cluster of people—neighbors—standing along the side of the road. We only had a handful of neighbors to begin with—what had happened to bring them all out onto the street? They spoke quietly among themselves, almost whispering, but suddenly one voice was clear: "It's just not right," it said. "What kind of world is it where things like *this* happen?"

Sensing my approach, the neighbors stepped apart, reminding me of scattering bowling pins. Part of me wanted to stop and ask, "What's not right? Things like what?" But by now, I could see my grandparents.

They were standing on their front lawn with one of the island sheriffs and two police officers. The three public officials were all talking on cell phones, and the two police officers were rifling through notepads. At least my grandfather was all right—but then what was all the commotion about?

No one was talking, but the police officers and the sheriff seemed incredibly busy, talking and rifling. My grandparents, by contrast, looked completely motionless, helpless, frozen in a block of ice.

Even as close as I was, as fast as I was moving, no one had noticed me yet.

"Grandma?" I said.

She immediately came to life, looking over at me, her face brightening.

"Zach!" my grandma said. "Where have you *been*? And—"

"—*where's your brother?*" my grandpa finished.

Everyone in the front yard immediately stopped talking and turned to look at me. All their eyes demanded a response.

Where's your brother?

For a moment, the question made no sense. It was a summer afternoon in July. Gilbert had to be around somewhere—with his friend Billy, maybe in their backyard, or down in my grandparents' cellar.

Wherever he was, he was *somewhere*.

Wasn't he?

"Grandma?" I said helplessly.

At this, my grandma's face looked like the sun during an eclipse as the moon slipped over the last slice of light. A second later, she and my grandpa froze solid again.

The police officers and the sheriff all converged on me. There were only three of them, but they suddenly seemed like news reporters at a press conference with the president, asking me a thousand questions.

"When did you last see him?"

"Do you have any idea where he might have gone?"

"Did he tell you this morning where he was planning on going today?"

I ignored them. "Grandma?" I said. "Grandpa? Where's Gilbert?"

But it was dumb question, because I knew my grandparents didn't know. It was obvious that Gilbert had disappeared, and no one, not my grandparents and not the police officers or sheriff, had any idea where he had gone.

———

Hours later, Gilbert still hadn't turned up.

All afternoon my grandparents had assumed that Gilbert was playing over at Billy's, just like I'd thought. But when they finally checked, they realized that Billy had been off-island with his mom for most of the day. I was kicking myself for being so quick to jump to the conclusion that Billy and his mother were back already. This was the problem with everyone assuming the island was so incredibly safe. If no one ever imagined that anyone could do anything bad—if no one ever locked their doors or kept their kids trapped behind chain-link fences—that made it that much easier when someone finally did.

Before they called the police, my grandparents had phoned the parents of all of Gilbert's other friends and checked every other house in the neighborhood. They checked the beach, the woods, the closest playground, and any other place they thought he might be.

The sheriff had arrived right away, but it had taken more than an hour for the police to arrive from the mainland on the ferry.

No one had seen Gilbert all day. I hadn't been the last person to talk to him—that had been my grandfather, who had made him lunch. Gilbert could've been missing since right after then.

I'd done my part, telling the police any place I could think of where he might be—even those big rocks on the beach out at Trumble Point, though I was sure he wouldn't go there by himself. But they wouldn't let me go and look for him—cell phone coverage was notoriously bad all over the island, and they said it was really, really important that we all be available to immediately answer any questions.

So all we could do was wait.

I'd never felt so completely helpless in my whole life. Pacing back and forth in our kitchen, I felt like a wild animal caged without tranquilizers, fearful and angry at the same time.

So after a while, I did what I always do when I feel helpless: I went upstairs to get online.

My brother is missing! I posted. *I think he's been kidnapped!*

When it became clear to my friends that I wasn't kidding, people started making suggestions.

You live on an island, MiniMimi wrote. *He has to be there somewhere!*

That's what the police believed too. They'd checked the security cameras at the ferry terminal and they hadn't seen him get on the boat. But if Gilbert had been kidnapped, it's not like they would've had him sitting with them in the front seat. They would have drugged him, or bound and gagged him, and put him in the back of a van.

And even now, the police *still* weren't searching the cars leaving the island. They said there were legal issues, that there was still no evidence that he'd actually been abducted.

This was all too complicated to post online. That's when I realized that while my friends could support me, they couldn't help me.

So I started searching for answers. I checked out the traffic cameras at the ferry terminals, available online, but they just had a bird's-eye view, not close enough to see inside any of the cars, and they were only showing the current shot anyway. There was no way for me to go back through the records and see what cars may have gotten on the ferry earlier in the day.

I searched in real time, looking for tweets or postings from anyone who might've seen my brother, or anyone looking like him, on the island or on the mainland. But I didn't find anything there, either.

So I started looking for more general information about child abductions, but that also wasn't any help.

Most of what I found just repeated what the police had already told us.

Before long, I realized the Internet couldn't help me find my brother.

Ninety percent of all missing kids turn up before their bedtime on the day they go missing, it had said on one website.

I looked at the clock. It was eight-thirty. Gilbert's bedtime was eight o'clock. It was already *past* his bedtime. If ninety percent of kids turned up before their bedtime, what happened to the other ten percent? Were they the ones who *never* turned up?

"No!" I said. I pushed myself away from my computer in frustration and spun around to face my room.

That's when I remembered the "special" incense in the drawer on my nightstand, the stuff I'd been given by that strange woman in the New Age shop.

6

Astral projection to find my missing little brother—now *that* was a stupid idea. It would *really* never work.

I glanced over at the shelf under my nightstand. That book, *Voyage Beyond the Rainbow*, the one I'd read the week when my grandparents had taken away my computer, was still there. What had Celestia Moonglow written—something about there being two planes of existence, with the astral plane looking into the material one? If that was true, I could look for Gilbert from the astral dimension. I could also leave the island.

Yeah, this was a stupid idea, and it probably wouldn't work. But what if it did? At this point, I had absolutely nothing to lose. I opened the drawer of my nightstand, and sure enough, the three sticks of incense were still there.

I found an incense stand in one of the drawers in my desk, then headed downstairs to make sure there hadn't been any new news about Gilbert. When there wasn't, I went back upstairs, lit the incense, and immediately settled back on the bed. I didn't bother with the candle or music this time.

The incense smoldered. Curious, I looked over at it. It burned differently than most incense, with the smoke almost dripping from the stick as if it was heavier than the air. But little by little, the smell of it filled the room.

Once again, it smelled good—at first. But after it burned for a minute or so, I detected that strange undercurrent, definitely something foul.

It smelled as thick as it looked, settling heavily inside my lungs, almost like a liquid.

I tried my best to ignore it. I started my breathing, inhaling, holding it, then letting it go. I didn't bother with the whole relaxation process that I'd done before: the breathing in and out, the exhaling the cares of the world. There was no way I'd be able to exhale the fact that my brother was missing.

Right away, something felt different. For one thing, I wasn't nearly so self-conscious. Suddenly, it didn't feel like

I was play-acting at something, with everything forced and calculated. This time it felt real.

And weirdly, in spite of everything that had happened with Gilbert, I also felt…*relaxed*. I felt calmer than I had in ages—definitely more than the first time I'd tried this astral projection thing. But it was more than just being relaxed. It was like I was now very aware of everything I was feeling and experiencing. At the same time, I had some distance—like the emotions were outside me somehow, and I could sit back and examine them, like white lace, intricate and fascinating.

Before I knew it, I was ready to begin the astral separation.

Eyes closed, I once again imagined a single point of light floating on my forehead. Even though the point was outside of me, I knew that it was part of myself, too, and that I had control over it.

The point of energy started to move, slowly drifting up, directly away from my head. I didn't remember consciously choosing to make the point move.

Six feet or so above me, the point stopped, floating effortlessly.

I knew it was now time for my mind and soul—every bit of me except for my physical body—to join that small, shimmering part of me.

I concentrated, even as the smoke from the incense kept dribbling down my throat into my lungs. I imagined my glowing spectral self levitating up off the bed and rising up to the point of light. In my mind's eye, it was happening. Now it was just a matter of making it happen for real.

I tried imagining it again, from start to finish.

But even as I was thinking this, I knew that I was still lying on the bed. Everything that was happening was only happening in my imagination.

It wasn't working. I wasn't going to be able to help Gilbert, not this way anyway. *Oh, well*, I thought. I'd known it wasn't real.

Maybe the incense was too thick, too overpowering. I decided to put the stick out, let the room clear for a bit, and then try it again.

I opened my eyes and sat upright in bed.

I looked down. My body was still lying back immobile on the bed. My *physical* body hadn't moved at all. It was my *spirit* that had sat upright.

It had worked.

It had worked!

The first thing I noticed was that my arms no longer hurt from rowing around all afternoon in that boat. I stared at myself lying down on the saggy bed. I could see my body, eyes closed, stretched out and peaceful, but it was nothing at all like looking in a mirror. This was no flat reflection—this was the real me: the ropy forearms, the mess of brown hair, the too-plump lips. I'd never seen my body from outside myself—never known the exact shape of my head or angle of my jaw—but even now, I didn't panic. My mind was still relaxed and focused. The whole experience felt alien, but also somehow familiar. It felt like I had done this before, maybe when dreaming.

A dream. That's what this had to be. I'd fallen asleep, or maybe I'd voluntarily entered some kind of dream state just like *Voyage Beyond the Rainbow* said. Except it didn't feel like any dream I'd had before. For one thing, I felt like I was awake—fully conscious, fully aware of myself, fully in control. That said, I felt somehow outside myself too, observing everything that was happening as if from the side.

The woman in the New Age store, the one who'd given me the incense, was right: this was no dream.

Only now did I notice that my mind—the part of me that had sat upright in bed—had a "body," too, sort of. It looked the same as the body down on the bed, with the same clothes. But it was translucent, glowing softly, like a ghost, or like the cheesy picture on the cover of *Voyage Beyond the Rainbow*. I still had a body, but I couldn't feel it—not my T-shirt clinging to my chest, or the waistband of my underwear, or the itchiness of my athlete's foot.

For the first time in my life, I was *outside* myself. I wasn't stuck in that sweaty, itchy, achy body.

It was disorienting, but it was also weirdly liberating. It actually *felt* like I was in two places at once. Except it was much more than that. I was suddenly aware that the boundaries that separate us, the feeling that our bodies stop where the rest of the world starts, are artificial—that we're all part of the greater world and there really is no boundary. The world is me, and I am it.

Mostly, I just felt free for the first time since my parents died.

I looked around the bedroom. The surroundings were the same—I was still in my dad's old bedroom at my grandparents' farmhouse on Hinder Island, with its creaky single bed and the faded *Poltergeist* movie poster on the wall. But things were different, too. For one thing, the room was darker, like there'd been a power outage and the lights had gone out.

I take that back. The lamp on the nightstand still glowed—it just burned as if through clouded glass. Celestia Moonglow said that the astral realm was a "shadow" dimension. I guess she'd meant that literally.

The sound was different, too. The sleepy silence of the island had been replaced by some kind of distant, steady roar, a cross between a moan and a hiss. The book hadn't said anything about this.

I looked back down at the me-on-the-bed. My body was completely motionless. Unconscious.

But *was* I unconscious? Everything that I'd ever been taught said that people's souls didn't just leave their bodies. *Not if they were still alive.*

It was like I suddenly remembered to panic. Now that I'd gotten my astral body out of my physical body, how did I get it back inside again?

I tried to inhale, to fight the panic that had filled me like a chest full of frozen water, but I couldn't get a breath. To hell with being one with the universe—there was no air in this place! I was going to suffocate.

I jerked back.

And suddenly I was lying in bed, back in the real world, body and soul reunited, dizzy and disoriented with aching biceps.

———

I had to try it again. Now that I was awake, I was immediately embarrassed that I'd panicked. Why had I wanted to breathe, anyway? I didn't need to breathe in a dimension where the physical didn't exist. Besides, Gilbert's life was at stake.

That incense had been quick-burning, or maybe I'd lost track of time. Either way, it had already burned its way down to the nub. So I lit a second stick and inhaled deeply, feeling it calm me. Then I worked my way through the visualizations, still breathing in and out. Finally, I imagined the point of light levitating in front of me.

And once again, I sat upright in bed. Once again, my spirit had detached from my physical body. It felt completely effortless.

My astral form climbed off the bed—or tried to anyway. There was no gravity in this astral dimension. Weirder still, my "body" seemed to have no real weight. It was like the bed was greased and I slid right off. I found myself flailing even as I hung in the air next to the bed, floating unsteadily, drifting slowly to the right.

Instinctively, I reached for the nightstand, but my hand passed right through it. If there'd been any doubt before about where I was, and that this really *was* a non-physical dimension, there wasn't now.

The astral dimension. I was really there—wherever or whatever "there" was. It was still dark and a little disorienting. But now I was getting used to the idea of it all.

And just as I'd suspected, I didn't need to breathe in this other place. The fact is, I *couldn't* breathe—there was no air to inhale. After a lifetime of doing that without thinking, this was the strangest thing of all. The first few times I tried to inhale and couldn't, I felt a flash of panic again. But when I didn't feel the effects of not breathing—no tightness in my neck and chest, no pounding blood racing to my head—it was surprising how quickly I got used to the idea.

I also couldn't blink—I couldn't even close my eyes. My eyes weren't my "eyes"—they weren't my way of seeing. I simply "saw" what was around me, even if the information still seemed to be coming in through my eyes.

As I kept floating there, I looked over at my body lying in bed. It was still bizarre to see myself, to be *outside* myself, but now that I was more mentally prepared, it didn't seem so scary. I was back to liking the way the whole experience made me feel, the sense of oneness and a growing giddiness about the possibility of it all.

As I looked at myself, I saw a faint line of silver light, like an umbilical cord, flowing out from behind the head of my physical body. About the width of a wrist, it spiraled out through the pillow, rising up and gently winding around to connect with the back of my spiritual head.

The silver cord. *Voyage Beyond the Rainbow* hadn't said anything about this, but I'd heard about it before, even if I couldn't think where. It was a line of energy that connected the astral body to the physical one.

I reached over to touch it. It was warm and soft, but pliable, like some kind of gel. I could run my hand all the way through it, and I felt a gentle pulse. It was only after I'd touched it that it occurred to me how strange it was that I could feel it at all. I'd passed my hand through the nightstand, but I hadn't been able to feel anything.

I reached over and felt my own astral arm. Sure enough, I *could* feel it, just as solid as in the real world—and much more solid than the silver cord. So I guess I was able to touch and feel things that were with me in the astral dimension.

By now, I'd stopped wobbling. Somehow I found my balance and was hanging motionless in the air. Suddenly the feeling of weightlessness didn't feel so uncontrollable. Suddenly I felt lighter than air, like I could fly.

I was in a non-physical realm, a world of the mind. That meant I didn't travel by physical means, but by mental ones: will power, not horsepower.

I imagined that I was the spot of light that had been hovering above my head. I let that spot float upward, and I began gently rising, too. All I had to do was will myself somewhere, and that's where I went. It was even easier than walking or riding a bike. Those things still involved the brain sending messages to the body—messages that weren't necessary in a place where the mind *was* the body.

I kept rising, like a human helium balloon with the silver cord for a string. I floated right through the ceiling, through a blackness that must have been the attic, and right out into the night sky.

It was even darker than it usually was on Hinder Island, so far away from the city lights of Tacoma and Seattle. In the astral dimension, the moon looked different—not just darker, but smudged, like a dirty paper lantern—but I could still see enough to make out up from down, and soon I'd even risen up to the treetops. I barely even noticed the height—what did it matter if you fell in a non-physical dimension anyway? Plus, I was still focused.

I thought about all that had happened in the last ten minutes: how my spirit had left my physical body and was rising upward like a balloon. But I wasn't panicking this time. Just like I'd quickly gotten used to the idea of not needing to breathe, I was getting used to the rest of it, too. Maybe all the time I'd spent online, traveling through the disembodied mind-world of cyberspace, had somehow prepared me for being outside myself in the astral world.

But the astral world was like cyberspace times a million. Here, you didn't just watch from a chair in your bedroom or the couch in your living room. Here, you were *there*.

Whether it was because of the incense or just the experience itself, my mind was still focused. I was experiencing all my emotions—especially the giddiness, the growing sense of possibility—but it was like I was outside those emotions too, like they were clouds overhead, and I could also watch them passing by.

I kept rising up, until I was far above the trees. At the same time, I was also moving slightly to the east, slowing drifting on some kind of vague ethereal breeze. I could see the mainland in the distance, the humming waterfront development that rimmed almost the entire Puget Sound like lace on a valentine. But it was mostly dark underneath me, just trees and water—a vast shadowy void in the center of a world of light.

I looked out over the world and thought, *From here, I can find Gilbert, no matter where in the world he is.*

And I was going to.

7

Celestia Moonglow had written that the astral dimension was a spiritual dimension, not a physical one. *Even distances don't exist in the way that they do in the material world,* she'd said.

I wasn't sure what this meant exactly, but it reminded me, once again, of the Internet. Distances didn't matter there, either—everything anywhere in the world was easily accessible with just a few clicks or touches.

I immediately thought about what I'd done when I was looking for Gilbert online: I'd done a search. I'd started with a text search, gradually narrowing down my parameters, but I'd also done video and photo searches.

I obviously couldn't do any of that here. But if distances didn't really matter, maybe I could *hear* Gilbert wherever he was. Maybe I could search for the sound of him.

So I listened.

I didn't hear anything at first, just the muffled moan/hiss that I'd heard the first time I'd entered this strange dimension.

Then a woman coughed.

Did that mean there was someone else nearby—some other astral traveler doing a little shadow-surfing before bed?

I heard something else: a cat's meow, long and plaintive. These noises sounded different than they might in the real world. They sounded hollow, with a slight echo, like they were coming from the bottom of a deep well. They definitely didn't sound like they were coming from directly around me.

A little girl squealed.

A man shouted at the top of his lungs.

A group of people recited the Pledge of Allegiance.

The more I listened, the more I heard. It was like doing an Internet search in the sense that I was getting an almost infinite number of results.

It was also a little like listening to the sounds of Hinder Island, each of them coming at you one by one. The difference was that I couldn't tell where they were coming from.

I could tell the direction of each one, but not the distance. That's when I realized that they were all coming from the astral roar—like it was made up of lots and lots of individual sounds and, when I listened closely, I was somehow able to distinguish them. But unlike on the island, I was only hearing the sounds of living things, not the sound of the wind blowing through the leaves or the jingling of the wind chimes.

A woman read a bedtime story.

A dog howled at the moon.

A girl sang "Amazing Grace" in German.

In German? I thought.

As I listened, I heard even more sounds. And just like an Internet search, most of it had nothing to do with what I was looking for.

I decided to expand my search parameters. I opened myself up wider, like a sail catching the wind, and the sounds kept coming. There were definitely other languages—Chinese, Spanish, and others I didn't recognize. Soon the voices were hardly recognizable as individual sounds, only a rising rumble of noise.

It continued to swell, even as it kept blending together. This wasn't like the sounds of the island at all—these were the sounds of a crowd. Soon it was overwhelming, and still it grew. I suddenly felt very small, not like I was one with the universe, but like I was standing in the middle of a vast ocean—in the hollow way things sounded, but also in the way everything *felt* around me. It was as if the trees and houses of Hinder Island didn't even exist. *Voyage Beyond the Rainbow* said the astral dimension was a separate plane of existence from the material dimension, and it was clearly true. But it was also a really *big* dimension, and it was like I could suddenly feel it stretching into eternity. So much for having a grip on my emotions. Suddenly, I wished this *was* a dream, so that I could wake up.

I clamped my hands over my ears. "Stop!" I said to the universe.

And even though I wasn't hearing the sounds through my ears, it worked: the noises stopped—all except for the distant, barren moan.

Gilbert. I needed to find my brother. But I couldn't just jump recklessly into the river of sound—that was too overwhelming. I had to deconstruct the roar, sorting through the noises like jelly beans, red and green and yellow and black and purple, looking for the elusive blue one.

So that's what I did, cautiously at first, being careful not to let them build, not to let it all overwhelm me.

But I still didn't hear Gilbert.

This is taking too long! I thought. If I had to sort through every noise in the astral dimension, I'd be there forever.

I needed to focus. I needed to listen for Gilbert, and Gilbert alone. What did he sound like? What noise would he be making right now?

That's when I heard it: the sniffle of a little boy.

Gilbert's sniffle. I was sure it was him. I'd recognize the sound of him anywhere. He was alive, at least.

But if I could hear him, maybe that meant he could also hear me.

"Gilbert!" I said to the breeze. "I'm here! Stay where you are—I'm coming to get you."

But how? Celestia Moonglow had said distances didn't exist in the astral dimension, but she hadn't said anything more about it. Most of the book had been about getting *into* the astral dimension—not what to do once you got there.

I could tell which direction the sound was coming from, just like in the physical world, so I started moving myself toward it.

It was slow at first, but soon I was flying across the sky like a wobbly Peter Pan. I flew south, past the lighthouse at Trumble Point, faintly glowing even in the astral dimension. Then I headed southeast right over Puget Sound.

Looking down, I realized there must have been a wind that night, because there were whitecaps in the water down below—choppy little peaks that glowed in the moonlight—rising, then collapsing again. But while there was a breeze in the astral dimension, it was that ethereal one, blowing in a different direction. I couldn't feel the real wind at all.

When I reached the mainland, I listened again. The city of Tacoma was on my left, up to the north, stretched out in a smoky glow. But I could hear that Gilbert was somewhere to the south—somewhere in the vast swath of darkness out past the lights of the city. That's the direction I turned.

I started moving horizontally across the sky, still unsteady, but less so. Because there was no friction in the astral dimension, the faster I flew, the faster I continued to fly. The windows of houses glowed below me, along with streetlights and headlights. But then I crossed over a freeway, and the glowing lights finally gave way to fields and forests, and I found myself mostly passing over the tips of dark, shaggy trees.

Before I knew it, I was many miles south of the urban area. By car, it would have taken me at least an hour to get here, but it had only been ten minutes as the crow—er, spirit—flies.

Gilbert's crying wasn't louder exactly, but somehow I knew it was closer. I slowed myself down.

Something flat and grey stretched out irregularly in the darkness up ahead—a lake, I realized. And nestled down below me along the shore of the lake, partially hidden by the dark spires of the forest, was a row of cabins. The lights were off in most of them, but not all of them.

Gilbert was inside one of the cabins with its lights on. I knew exactly which one. There was a white SUV parked out front.

I didn't think, just swooped down to the cabin, then through the roof, right inside.

———

It was only a little lighter inside than it had been outside. A fixture hung above a round dinner table, burning dimly.

But there was enough light to see I'd been right: Gilbert sat sniffling at the dinner table. His feet and hands were tied, and the chest of his T-shirt was wet with snot and tears.

"Gilbert!" I said, literally flying to his side. He really had been kidnapped, but at least now I knew what had happened to him. "It's okay. I'm here now."

But when I bent down to untie my brother, my hands passed right through his legs exactly the way my body had passed through buildings. I still wasn't completely used to the astral dimension.

"Damn it," I said. I knew what had happened to Gilbert, but there wasn't anything I could do about it. I saw now that the astral dimension wasn't better than cyberspace in every respect. There you had at least *some* influence in the real world. Here you were in a completely separate place, unable to affect things at all.

My brother kept sniffling.

"Gilbert!" I said. "It's me—Zach. I found you!"

He didn't react. He didn't even know I was there.

"Gilbert, listen to me! Everything's going to be all right. Just hold tight." I didn't want to leave my brother alone again, but I knew I needed to go get help.

Right then, someone stepped into the front room of the cabin from a room separated by swinging doors—the kitchen. It was an older woman in a dark coat—one of those former-model types with a too-taut face and hair that was too blond for her age. She was the kind of person who might be seen on Hinder Island for a weekend or so, staying in one of the high-end bed-and-breakfasts, but she'd never live there. She carried a glass of water that she placed on the table in front of Gilbert.

The kidnapper.

"There you go," she said to Gilbert. "I'm sorry I can't untie you, but I think you can still hold it, can't you?"

Gilbert just started crying harder.

"What are you doing with my little brother?" I shouted at her.

But of course she didn't respond, just kept looking sadly at Gilbert. She couldn't hear me either.

"Everything's going to be okay," she said to him gently. "I promise."

"It's not going to be okay!" I said. "Not unless you take him back home!"

She hesitated.

Suddenly a second person stuck his head into the front room from the kitchen, a man talking on a cell phone. He was older than the woman, probably in his sixties. His teeth were almost blindingly white, and his hair just as unnaturally dark as the woman's was blond.

"Evelyn!" he snapped at the woman. "Would you please shut him the hell up for just one minute?"

"I'm *trying*," the woman—Evelyn—said. "But your shouting isn't helping any."

"Yes, I'm still here," the man said into the cell phone. "No, he's fine. He just won't stop crying."

"How about a cookie?" Evelyn said to Gilbert. "I bet you'd like a cookie. No, wait, we don't have any. How about some Melba toast?"

Gilbert just kept crying.

"I don't understand!" I said, even though I knew no one could hear me. "Why did you kidnap *Gilbert?*" I'd never seen either of these people before.

Evelyn hesitated again. She glanced over in my direction.

What was this? I'd just assumed that no one could hear me in the real world, but maybe I was wrong.

"Can you hear me?" I said.

She didn't seem to. Instead, she tried another approach with Gilbert. Spotting the crystal centerpiece in the middle of the table, she pushed it closer to Gilbert. "Look at this," she said in a softer voice. "Isn't it pretty? It's Waterford."

"I know what you did!" I shouted at Evelyn. "I know you kidnapped my little brother, and I'm going to tell the police! What do you think about *that?*"

Meanwhile, the crystal centerpiece actually seemed to get Gilbert's attention. He was still crying, but it was back to a sniffle now. Even though his hands were still tied, he reached for the crystal.

"*Stop!*" Evelyn said, suddenly horrified. "I didn't say you could *touch* it, did I?"

Gilbert burst out bawling.

I floated closer to Evelyn so I could talk right in her ear.

"I know you can hear me," I said, my voice rising. "When I turn you in, you're going to rot in jail. Did you hear *that*? Rot in *jail*."

Evelyn turned toward me. I think she was scowling, but it was hard to tell given all the work she'd had done on her face. Still, it seemed like she was about to say something.

Instead, she stepped forward, walking right through me.

I felt a tingle up and down my whole body. It wasn't strong, like that scene in the movie *Ghost* where the wife walks through the ghost of her dead husband, and he's overcome by her essence. It felt more like I'd walked through a spider's web. Still, I felt *something*. What did that mean—that you *could* impact the physical world from the astral one? Of course Celestia Moonglow hadn't said anything about any of this.

"Uh huh," the man was saying into the phone, having returned from the kitchen. "Uh huh. Yes, definitely—we'll meet you there." He cut off the call and looked over at Evelyn, glaring at her. "Do you think you could have been a little *louder*?"

Evelyn ignored him. She was pacing back and forth in the front room. "My God, Conrad. What have we done?"

"You kidnapped my little brother!" I said. "That's what you did! And when the police find you, you're both going to *fry!*"

"We did what we had to do," Conrad said to her. "We didn't have any choice."

"No choice?" I shouted. "Of *course* you had a choice! And you *still* have a choice—you can take Gilbert home right now."

Suddenly a teenager stepped into the room from the opposite side of the cabin. There was a third kidnapper? Conrad and Evelyn had brought their teenage son?

"They can't hear you," the guy said. He was looking right at me.

"What?" I said, confused. "You can see me?"

"Sure. I'm not with them. I'm here with you."

It took me a second to make sense of this, but as I stared at the guy, I realized how different he looked from the others. He was glowing like me.

He wasn't a third kidnapper. He was with me in the astral realm.

8

"Wait," I said to the guy floating across from me. "You can really see me? You're really here?"

"In the flesh," the guy said. "Well, not really, but you know what I mean." His voice sounded different than the ones I was hearing from the real world—clearer, more solid. We were both on the same side of the looking glass, I guess.

"I heard you shouting," he said. "I came to see what all the commotion was."

"I wasn't shouting." But of course I had been—at Conrad and Evelyn.

I had no idea what question to ask him first. Then I realized I didn't have time to ask any questions at all.

"This is my brother," I said quickly, nodding at Gilbert. "He's been kidnapped. I came into the astral dimension to find him, and I did, but now I have to tell the police where he is."

As the guy glanced over at Gilbert, I looked at him. He was at least half-Asian, but with pale skin. He reminded me of an elf, someone elusive and mysterious—though how much of that had to do with the fact that I was seeing him in spirit form, I didn't know. I doubted the confidence on his face, the aura of brashness about him, had anything to do with being in the astral realm.

"You live around here?" I said.

"Not really," he said. "It's probably, like, twenty miles." He nodded back, in pretty much the opposite direction I'd come from. Only now did I notice the faint silver cord flowing out of the back of his head, too. It gently spiraled off into the shadows, but it was a lot thinner than the one I'd seen from my own head. That said, when I looked back at my own cord, it was thinner now, too, less than half an inch wide—even thinner than the guy's in front of me. It was as if there was only so much material to the cords, and the farther they were stretched, the thinner they became, like gum. I wondered if they'd snap if you went too far.

"I'm Emory," the guy said. "Like the fingernail board."

"Zach," I mumbled, even as I thought how I needed to get home and call the police. "Oh, hell!" I said, thinking out loud. "I don't even know where we are!"

"Silver Lake."

I looked at him. "What?"

"We pass it on the road all the time. I don't live *that* far away."

"But I saw different cabins. The police won't know which one he's in."

"It's okay," Emory said. "There's probably an address out on the mailbox."

This was a good idea. I turned and flew right through the wall, out to the gravel driveway and the mailbox out by the street. The numbers were white and reflective, and they glowed in the moonlight, even in the shadow of the astral dimension.

924, it said.

"But what's the name of the road?" I was already panicking again.

"Silver Lake Road," Emory said. He'd followed me out through the wall. "924 Silver Lake Road," he repeated.

I turned toward him. We both hovered, glowing in the dark. "Have you been here before?" I said. "The astral dimension?"

"Maybe. Why?"

"I need to get home fast."

"Use the silver cord."

"The silver cord?"

"Let it pull you home," Emory said. "That's how I do it. It's much faster that flying. Almost instantaneous."

"What do you mean let it pull me home?"

"You just ... relax. The silver cord will pull you right back to your body. It's like...falling asleep. But you have to relax. You have to let it happen."

Now that he'd said this, I remembered that this is what had happened the very first time I'd entered the astral realm, when I'd panicked. But relax? Now?

I looked at Emory. "Will you do it, too? Go back to your body and wake up and call the police?"

He nodded. "Sure. If you want me to."

"If they hear the same address from two people, there's no way they won't listen." Besides, I had no idea if this silver cord thing was going to work, and it was a long way back to Hinder Island.

"I'll go right now," Emory said. "924 Silver Lake Road," he said one final time. Then I watched his eyes lose focus and watched his body hang motionless in the air, leaning back slightly. The silver cord coming out of the back of his head throbbed and buckled slightly.

Suddenly his body whipped away. One second, he was there, the next second he was gone. It was so fast that it looked like it would be painful. But I reminded myself that it hadn't been his body at all—that we were in the non-physical astral dimension.

I had no idea if Emory would actually call the police. He'd said he would, and he'd seemed trustworthy, but I didn't know anything about him.

I needed to do it, too. I needed to use my own silver cord to get back to my house on Hinder Island so I could tell my grandparents and the police what I'd learned.

I couldn't close my eyes, so I just hung there, thinking about home, willing myself to be reunited with my body. I tried to remember how I'd felt before, relaxed and centered by the meditation and the incense.

But nothing happened. I'd long since lost the grip on my emotions.

You have to relax, Emory had said. *You have to let it happen.*

I couldn't relax. Not now. But somehow I had to let go anyway.

I kept concentrating. I tried to duplicate the breathing I'd done before. But I didn't need to breathe, so that just felt awkward now.

Still nothing happened. But I kept trying—my spirit was meant to be inside my body, so I knew it couldn't be *that* hard to get them back together.

Finally, I felt my mind growing foggy, felt my body slowly turning so the back of my head, with the silver cord, was facing the way I wanted to be traveling. It was all very gentle. Somehow I knew that I'd wink away at any second, but I was more relaxed now, so it didn't scare me.

Just then I felt a familiar chill, a shiver up and down my body, like what I'd felt that day out at Trumble Point. The difference was that I didn't have a body now. So how could I feel the cold? Maybe this was part of the travel-by-silver-cord. But if so, why did I get that same feeling that something terrible was going to happen?

At the same time, I felt my body begin to slip away, like I was starting backward down the slope of a steep water slide. As I was being pulled away, I caught the vaguest flash of something out of the corner of my eye, like it was coming down right over my head.

It had to be a trick of the light, a stray shadow. But the truth is it almost looked like some kind of black tentacle.

———

I opened my eyes—my physical eyes. I was back in my bedroom at my grandparents' farmhouse on Hinder Island. It all happened in an instant.

It was a shock, waking up back in the real world. It wasn't at all like waking up from sleep. That's when you rest your mind. But my mind hadn't been at rest—it had completely left my body, and now had to reintegrate itself back in.

My body was still alive, and it had kept on breathing while I was gone. Now I had to synch my mind back up with that breathing. But I'd gone so long without breathing in the astral dimension that it was like I was fighting my body's involuntary reflex. It was all I could do not to choke. I'd even forgotten the impulse to blink.

Then there was gravity; it was so much heavier than I remembered! And my clothing was tighter, and any itches I felt were stronger too. In a way, it was harder to go from the astral dimension to the real world than it had been to go into the astral dimension in the first place, which was ironic because I'd spent my whole life inside my body.

I ignored all that. What I had to tell the police was far more important than any disorientation or irritation I was feeling.

I thundered down the stairs of my grandparents' house. "Grandma! Grandpa! I know where Gilbert is!"

My grandparents had been in the kitchen talking to a police officer, but they met me in the front hallway. My grandpa clutched the handle of a coffee mug in his hand, but he was holding it horizontally, like he'd spilled the contents in his mad rush to get to me.

"You *do?*" my grandma asked. "Zachary, why didn't—"

"—you tell us before?" my grandpa said. Even now, they were still finishing each other's sentences.

"I didn't *know* before!" I said. "I just found out!"

"Where is he?" the police officer said.

"He's being held in a cabin out on Silver Lake, about an hour south of Tacoma!" I told her the exact address.

"How do you know this?" the officer asked me.

That's the moment I saw the problem with my plan. I couldn't very well tell my grandparents and the police officer the truth. They'd never believe me.

"Someone online," I said. "I posted a picture of Gilbert, and someone said they saw someone who looked just like him being carried into this cabin on Silver Lake Road."

I was proud of myself—I'd come up with a pretty good lie, right there on the spot.

My grandparents both turned to the police officer.

"You have to send somebody!" my grandpa said.

"You have to see if he's there!" my grandma said.

The officer looked at me. "Can you show me this email?"

Maybe this isn't such a good lie, I thought.

"It wasn't an email," I said. "It was an IM message. And I didn't save it—I have my settings set so my computer doesn't save them. I should've saved it!"

"It's okay. But can I talk to whoever sent it to you?" Even now she was starting for the stairs.

"It wasn't anyone I know. I just posted Gilbert's picture in this local forum, and someone saw it, and they just IM'd me out of the blue." I stopped. The policeman just stared at me. "But it was real, and I know that's the right address. You have to send someone out there!"

"Yes!" my grandma said. "Please!"

The officer looked from me to my grandparents, all our eyes filled with the same desperation and hope. Then finally she said, "924 Silver Lake Road? Sure, I'll call it in. But I wouldn't get your hopes up too high. Whenever word of a kidnapping gets out, we always get a lot of calls like these, and almost all of them turn out to be either pranks or cases of mistaken identity."

Maybe so, I thought, *but this is definitely no mistake.*

Then I exhaled for what felt like the first time since I'd entered the astral realm at least a half hour before.

9

I told my grandparents and the police officer that I was going to see what else I could find on my computer. Then I ran up to my room to light another stick of incense— my last one. Sure, the officer had said they were going to check out the cabin—but would they really do it? I needed to know for sure. And I needed to be with Gilbert, at least in the astral dimension, until they got there.

Once in the astral realm again, I immediately listened for Gilbert.

I didn't hear him. I heard women laughing, couples arguing, even monks chanting. But I didn't hear Gilbert. Suddenly my Internet-like astral search was getting no good returns at all.

I tried again, but no matter how hard I strained, no matter how many sounds I sorted through, I couldn't hear him. No whimpering, no soft breathing. As I flipped my way through the sounds, I heard plenty of crying, even lots of kids. But none of them were Gilbert.

"Gilbert, where *are* you?" I said, sending out my own astral text message. But I got no response.

I hadn't counted on this. I'd just assumed that since I'd heard him before, I'd be able to hear him again.

What did this mean? That he'd finally stopped crying? Or—?

No. I couldn't go there.

Conrad and Evelyn. I could listen for *them*.

I tried, hard.

Nothing.

I tried them one at a time. I tried them together. I tried them in every way that I could think of.

Still nothing.

So I had no choice but to try to retrace the route I'd taken before to the cabin out on Silver Lake.

I rose up over Hinder Island. Once again guiding myself by the lighthouse at Trumble Point, I flew south across the water. The whitecaps were gone now. The bay looked black and heavy from behind the astral lens, like thick crude oil.

I reached the mainland. I knew Silver Lake was beyond the urban area, many miles to the south, so I headed in that direction. But it was different than before, that effortless glide I'd managed while honing in on Gilbert's crying. This time I couldn't let go. This time I was searching visually, so I had to be slow, always keeping an eye on the shadowy landmarks below me.

And once I left the lights of greater Tacoma behind, the landmarks got murkier—much murkier.

In the dark of the night, and in the shadows of the astral dimension, everything below me looked the same: a black, choppy sea of fir tree tops. When I'd been traveling this way before, I'd been paying attention to the sound of Gilbert, not to physical landmarks.

Before I knew it, I was lost.

I stared down at the ocean of blackness that stretched out under me in all directions. I had no idea which was the right way, but if I chose wrong, Gilbert was lost to me. Even as I thought this, I sensed myself sliding, blown aimlessly along by that ever-present ethereal breeze.

I looked up into the sky. From the astral dimension, it looked even darker than normal country sky. And yet, because of those faded pinpricks of starlight, it was still lighter than the swath of forested darkness below.

I rocketed straight up into the sky.

And just when I reached the point when I started to see the curvature of the black earth below me, I caught a glimpse of something flat in the distance, glistening like tarnished silver.

A lake.

———

I found the cabin again, but the SUV wasn't in the driveway, and it looked like the lights had been turned off.

Please don't let them be gone, I thought.

I flew down through the ceiling of the cabin. Without light it was a tank of black ink. It occurred to me for the first time that no matter how much time I spent in the astral dimension, my eyes never adjusted to the dark.

Still, it had taken me a long time to find this cabin again. Maybe the police had already come and taken them away.

"Zach?" a voice said.

I jumped. It was Emory, floating next to me in the shadows.

"I thought you said you were going to call the police!" I said.

"I did," he said, wavering, taken aback by my anger.

But even as I said this, I realized the stupid mistake I'd made. When I'd gone to call the police, I should've had Emory stay here with Gilbert. At the time I hadn't been sure that I'd be able to get back to Hinder Island fast enough, but it had been more important not to lose track of Gilbert.

"By the time I got back here, they were gone," he said.

"How long ago was that?"

"I don't know. Twenty minutes?"

I thought back on how long it had been since we'd told the police what we'd learned. If Emory had been here for twenty minutes, there wasn't enough time for the police to have come and found Gilbert and taken them all away.

I listened, not for Gilbert, but for any sound around me. I didn't hear a thing. Somehow I just knew that the cabin was empty. Conrad and Evelyn had taken Gilbert somewhere else. But where? It was too dark in the cabin to even look for clues.

"Zach?" Emory said. "Do you feel something? Something not quite right?"

"My brother is gone, and I'm floating like a ghost in the astral dimension!" I said. "*Everything* feels not quite right."

"No, I mean something else."

I ignored him. Suddenly I flew straight up through the roof, into the sky, up to the point again where I'd been able to see the curvature of the earth. I scanned the horizon for the white SUV I'd seen parked in the driveway before.

I saw a few sets of headlights cutting through the gloom, and a few more sets of red tail-lights. But most were far, far away, and they were all traveling in opposite directions. If

Conrad and Evelyn had left more than twenty minutes ago, they'd be long gone by now.

"Anything?" Emory said. He'd followed me up into the sky and was now looking over the landscape with me.

"No," I said. As irritated as I'd sounded with him, I was actually glad to have him around. At least it meant I wasn't alone. And the way he hung next to me in the sky was reassuring somehow. He seemed steadier, more solid, not hanging loosely in the sky like me, but actually standing in it, like a floating statue of a sentinel. "How many times have you been here," I asked him.

"You asked me that before," he said. "A few times. Why?"

"I've never been here before tonight." I was embarrassed that I'd needed that stupid incense, but for some reason, I decided to tell Emory the truth about that, too. "What about you?" I asked him. "How'd you get here?"

"Same way you did," he said. "With that weird incense."

It was an interesting coincidence if it was true—but something told me it wasn't. But if he hadn't used the incense, I wondered how he'd gotten here. Celestia Moonglow and the woman at the New Age store had both seemed to agree that without the incense, you could only get here partway, experiencing as if through a dream. Emory didn't look like he was dreaming. Then again, I wasn't sure I'd be able to tell the difference.

I heard car tires on gravel down below us. Headlights shone on the cabin—a car had pulled into the driveway.

They're back, I thought.

I swooped back down to the cabin.

But it wasn't Gilbert and his kidnappers—it was a police car. They were coming to check out the cabin, following up on the tip Emory and I had reported. That was something, at least.

It was two male officers, one skinny, one fat. That was all I could make out in the veiled moonlight.

"Where are we again?" the fat one said. "The meth lab or the missing kid?"

"The missing kid," the skinny one said. "They had a couple reports that someone saw him here."

"Doesn't look like there's anyone home."

"Yeah, they're gone," I said to the cops. "But there might be a clue inside. And you can also look to see who owns this cabin. They're the ones who have my brother."

Emory had followed me down. "Zach," he said, "they can't hear you."

I didn't know that for sure. I didn't see how it hurt to *try* talking to them.

"Let's check it out," the skinny cop said to the fat one.

They left their headlights on, bathing the front of the cabin in light, then walked up to the front door and knocked. When no one answered, the skinny cop knocked again, louder, and called, "Hello? Is anyone home?"

Finally the skinny cop said, "This is the police! If there's anyone in there, we'd like to talk to you, please!"

Still no one came to the door.

"Just go inside!" I shouted at them, but of course they ignored me.

Instead, they started walking around the house, shining their flashlights into the windows. There were no curtains in the kitchen, so they were able to poke their beams inside.

"I don't think there's anyone here," the fat cop said.

"Looks that way," the skinny cop said.

"I'll call it in."

Then they started back toward the car.

"Wait!" I said. "You're not done, are you?" I looked over at Emory. "They're not done, are they? They need to look for evidence—search for fingerprints."

"I don't think they can," Emory said. "Not without a warrant. They need some kind of probable cause, and all they have is two anonymous tips."

I ignored him and spoke directly to the police. "Wait! Stop!"

But they just kept walking. Then they climbed into their car and drove away.

"Well, they're still going to look and see who owns the cabin, right? They'll trace them that way, right?"

"Zach, I don't know."

"Well, we can wait," I said. "Conrad and Evelyn probably just went to get groceries or something. We can wait here until they get back, and then we can call the police again."

But that didn't make sense; they wouldn't have both gone to get groceries, not with a kidnapped kid. He could scream in the supermarket. And even as I thought this through, I remembered how Conrad had been talking on his cell phone and had said something about meeting someone. I told Emory this.

"That's where they must've taken Gilbert," he said. "To meet a plane or boat?"

I didn't like the sound of that—there had to be dozens of private airports in the Puget Sound area, and hundreds of marinas. Still, it made sense.

"We need to listen for him again," I said.

We listened. But I still didn't hear anything.

"Emory?" I asked hopefully.

He shook his head.

"What does that *mean*?" I said. "I heard him before. Why can't I hear him now?"

"Zach, he's fine. I'm sure of it. They wouldn't have kidnapped him in the first place if they were just going to kill him."

I hadn't expected him to say the word "kill". My head started to swim. For a second, I thought I was going to throw up. Without a body, I didn't know how that was even possible.

"Conrad and Evelyn, then," I said. "We need to listen for *them*." It was as if by pretending I hadn't already tried this, I might get a completely different result.

But I didn't get a different result. I still couldn't hear them, and neither could Emory.

"I don't understand," I said. "We can't hear *them*, either? What happened?" I thought back on that book *Voyage Beyond the Rainbow*, but of course she hadn't said anything about any of this.

"Maybe it's because you know Gilbert," Emory said. "He's your brother. But we only heard Conrad and Evelyn that one single time."

This made a kind of sense. But it still made me angry.

"What is going *on?*" I shouted. "Not just the astral stuff—how could they've taken him in the first place? Gilbert knows not to talk to strangers. If someone he didn't know had tried to grab him, he would've screamed bloody murder."

"So maybe Conrad and Evelyn weren't strangers," Emory said.

I shook my head so hard it made my whole body sway. "I told you, I've never seen them before."

"Okay, so maybe it wasn't Conrad and Evelyn who grabbed him. Maybe it was someone else who handed him off to them. Someone he trusted. Someone dressed like a policeman."

What Emory was saying made sense. The person who did the kidnapping wasn't always the person the kid ended up with. I'd read this online. Kids got traded off all the time—which is what made it that much harder to trace them.

"But there are no policemen on Hinder Island," I said. "Just two sheriffs. There are no strangers either. Everyone is—"

I stopped mid-word. An idea was dawning on me like the moon breaking through clouds.

Emory looked at me. "What is it?"

"I think I know who might've taken Gilbert off the island."

10

I told Emory about the woman at the New Age store, the one who'd sold me the special incense. "She knew all about Gilbert—his name and everything!" I said.

"But I thought you said everyone knew everyone on the island," he said.

"They do, but Gilbert wasn't even with me at the time. And that's not even the weird part. She had this really big purse, like a carpet bag—that's where she kept the 'special' incense. A couple of weeks earlier, Gilbert and I were out at this park, and I saw he had this candy, and I asked who had given it to him, and he told me the lady with the really big purse. It *had* to be her. Plus, she was just kinda weird."

I didn't tell Emory this, but she had also been willing to sell me that incense, something pretty obviously illegal or illicit. It was clear she wasn't the most ethical person.

"A strange woman gives a kid candy, and a couple of weeks later, he turns up missing?" Emory said. "I'd say that's a definite lead. You should go back and tell the police. Everyone knows adults aren't supposed to give candy to kids they don't know."

"Yeah! No, wait." I thought for a second. "I don't have any more incense."

"So?"

"So what if I'm wrong? What if it wasn't her? I wouldn't be able to get back in the astral dimension again." The woman in the New Age shop wasn't going to give me more of that special incense, not if I reported her to the police. And even if she *was* willing, where was I going to get $100 cash?

"What are you saying?" Emory asked.

"I'm saying I want to check her out first, see if she really did have any connection to the kidnapping—check her out from the astral dimension, I mean. If I find anything, *then* I can call the police."

"Are you sure?"

"Yes, I'm sure!" I snapped at him. I stopped myself. I had one friend in the astral realm—did I really want to piss him off? "Sorry. Look, is there any chance you'd be willing to come with me?"

"I guess." He glanced at the shadows around us. "The truth is, something about this place is kinda creeping me out."

I wasn't sure if he meant the cabin or the whole astral dimension. But I was focused on other things, so I didn't bother to ask.

———

We started flying back to Hinder Island together. I didn't dare do that whole weird silver cord thing again. For one thing, Emory and I couldn't do it together. But more importantly, I didn't see how I could let it draw me back to my body and not have it end with me suddenly waking up.

We reached Puget Sound sooner than I expected. It's a long, narrow body of water that runs deep into the state. We must have cut directly across the mainland and caught up with it south of Hinder Island. But Puget Sound has lots of islands and peninsulas, and in the astral dark, they all looked more or less the same. I was starting to think I'd never get home.

Then I caught sight of a soft glow of light farther up the Sound—the lighthouse at Trumble Point. I'd never been so happy to see anything to do with Hinder Island.

With the lighthouse in sight, I started to pick up speed. By this point, I could fly pretty fast, but I wasn't as fast as Emory. I'd been like a wobbly Peter Pan before, and even now I was barely managing a serviceable hang glide, while he looked like Superman, confident and a little exaggerated.

He seemed to sense me watching him. "Do you know where she lives?" he said, slowing down to my speed. "The woman in the New Age shop?"

I thought back to the New Age shop. I was pretty sure there was an apartment in the back of the store.

"I think so," I said.

———

We landed in the street in front of the store. I hadn't been looking, and suddenly a car, headlights looming, swept right through us.

I flinched, surprised. But Emory didn't. Now I was almost certain he'd been in the astral dimension more than once or twice before.

I was still a little disoriented from the car, but I turned and looked at the New Age shop.

Emory reached over and touched me on the shoulder with a finger.

I jumped, startled again. Just that small push made me slide sideways a few inches in the frictionless astral dimension, until I stopped myself with my mind. He had only touched me for a second, and he hadn't touched me on bare "skin," but on my "shirt." But I'd felt him anyway, clearly, and in a way that was much more intimate than just touching bare skin. It was like he'd brushed against something deeper, something inside me, and it made me tingle.

"Why'd you do that?" I said.

Emory thought about it. "To see if I could feel you," he said at last. "I'd been wondering. I mean, I know we're just spirits or whatever. But I can feel my own body. So I was wondering if I could feel you, too, or if my hand would pass right through."

Feel me? Maybe he hadn't been lying about only coming to the astral dimension once or twice before.

"For the record, I could," he said, even as he looked away, embarrassed. "Feel you."

I could feel you, too, I thought, just as embarrassed. It wasn't just the touch itself, but the little tingle of electricity, of energy. I'd never felt anything quite like it in my life.

"So this is the New Age shop, huh?" he said, changing the subject.

"Yeah," I said. The lights were off.

As he peered in through the darkened windows, I snuck another look at him. For the first time since meeting him, I realized how cute he was. But as I watched him now, I thought I saw the confident mask slip a little, revealing a layer of sadness underneath.

I couldn't help but wonder, *Is he like me?*

Suddenly *he* flinched.

"What is it?" I said, looking to see if there was another car coming. But this late at night, the street was dark.

Emory glanced at the shadows around us. It was like he shivered. "I don't know. It just feels like it did out at the cabin. Like we're being watched."

Watched? He hadn't said anything before about being watched. By who?

I remembered that familiar chill I'd felt out at the cabin on Silver Lake, right before I'd seen what had looked like some kind of black tentacle. But that had just been a trick of the shadows.

"I thought I saw something out there," I said. In all the excitement, I'd forgotten to mention this to Emory.

The whites of his eyes looked unnaturally bright in the astral dark. "Something? Like what?"

If you'd seen it too, you'd know what I mean, I thought.

"Forget it," I said. "Let's just go inside."

———

The front door was glass with a sign taped to it that displayed the hours of the store. I floated right through them, into the area inside.

It looked very different in the dark—none of the bright colors from before, everything shades of grey—and the ceiling seemed lower than I remembered. There had been lots of different smells before, too, but of course I couldn't smell anything now.

"Let's see if there's an apartment in the back like you thought," Emory said, pressing forward, wafting through the counters and shelves.

I followed him and suddenly found myself passing right through the hexagonal glass case with the crystal figurines.

The light had been out before, making the figurines look drab, but ironically, they were catching the moonlight now and even sparkling. Gliding forward, I was impaled by the crystal unicorn.

I shivered, suddenly cold again.

I kept moving forward, all the way to the back of the store. The beaded curtain to the back room was tightly closed. I scanned the wall in front of me.

Eyes stared back at me.

I jerked back in surprise. I had no pulse to pound, no heart to catch in my throat, but I couldn't remember ever being so startled.

Swaying unsteadily, I looked again.

It was a mirror—one of the colorful African ones I'd seen covering the wall all those weeks before. I must have caught sight of my own my face in its reflection. I had glimpsed my own eyes.

But as I looked more closely at the mirrors, I didn't see my own face or eyes reflected in any of them now. And I take back what I said about seeing my own eyes; I couldn't have. I was in the astral dimension, but the mirror was in the physical dimension. Even if I'd happened to look into the mirror, it wouldn't have reflected anything.

So what had I seen? Was this what Emory had been talking about when he said it felt like he was being watched? But by who?

It's nothing, I thought. Another trick of the moonlight. I hadn't really seen anything.

I looked for Emory, but he'd already disappeared through the back wall.

"Emory?" I said, still uneasy.

He immediately floated back out into the store. "What is it?"

"Oh," I said, startled again. "I, um, just wondered where you went."

"For the record," he said, "there is an apartment back here." He turned back toward it.

Emory was still there with me. I wasn't alone. Everything was fine.

I followed him through the wall with the mirrors, but I made a point not to touch any of them with my astral body.

The light in the room beyond the wall caught me by surprise. I can't say it was bright—from the astral dimension, it was still like I was wearing dark glasses. But it had come so suddenly, and I'd been in the darkness for so long, that I found myself disoriented.

The apartment was small—a kitchenette and a front room with what looked like a single bedroom to one side—and it definitely wasn't glamorous, with none of the fountains or Himalayan rugs from the store in front. But it was neat.

Someone was lying on the couch watching television—a crime procedural.

"Is that her?" Emory said.

"Yeah," I said. Even now, I expected her to look up at us and scream. She was wearing a bathrobe with socks, not slippers, and her hair was wet from the shower.

"I gotta say," he said, "she doesn't look like a kidnapper."

I didn't say anything, but I couldn't disagree.

Emory looked around the apartment, but I couldn't stop looking at the woman from the store. Had she really kidnapped my little brother and handed him off to Conrad and Evelyn?

She picked her ear.

"What exactly are we looking for?" Emory said at last.

"Some evidence that ties her to the kidnapping." But now I saw the problem: even if she was involved, it's not like she was going to have a lock of Gilbert's hair stuck to her refrigerator.

"I'm going to check the bedroom—and see if there's a garage," Emory said. "Maybe she left something in her car."

I nodded, and he disappeared through one of the walls. I kept staring at the woman from the store. For some reason, I couldn't look away. I'd made it all the way to this astral dimension where I'd also been able to "hear" my brother from dozens of miles away. Who's to say I couldn't also read this woman's mind?

I decided just to ask her. "Did you take him?" I said. "Did you kidnap my little brother?" If anyone could hear me, it would be a woman who worked in a New Age store.

She yawned and just kept watching television.

This wasn't getting me anywhere.

I was just about to join Emory in the other room when her cell phone rang. I froze. This wasn't reading her mind exactly, but it could still be valuable information, depending on who was on the other end of the line. Maybe it was Conrad and Evelyn calling.

She answered her phone. "Hello?" She listened, then leaned back again on the couch. "Oh, hey, what's up?" She listened some more. "Oh, God, I wish!"

It didn't sound like she was talking to people she'd been hired to kidnap for. But even if it was just a relative or friend, she could still say something important.

"Not a word," she said into the phone. "And you know what really burns me up about that? He was the one who said he wanted to go so bad! I told him it wasn't a good time, that I didn't have anything to wear. But he *begged* me!"

This was *really* getting me nowhere. And if she really had kidnapped Gilbert this afternoon, she had to be the world's most heartless person to be so cool about it now.

"Oh, things are picking up," she said. "Every year I say, 'That's it—I'm done! Things are never going to pick up.' But they do, they always do. It's never Memorial Day weekend, which is another thing I always think. It's Fourth of July. It's like no one can take a vacation before then, not even a weekend. But I had a great day today—so good I missed my shows!"

She was telling her friend she'd worked in the store all day. Gilbert had been kidnapped sometime after noon. I thought back to the sign I'd seen in the window of the door, the one that gave the store hours. It said the store opened at ten. If what this woman was saying now was true, she couldn't have taken Gilbert, not unless she'd locked up the store for at least an hour—and that was assuming that Conrad and Evelyn had met her somewhere on the island and she didn't have to take the ferry to the mainland and back. But that didn't make any sense—Conrad and Evelyn weren't islanders. They'd have to know they'd draw attention on an island like this in the middle of the week. That was the last thing they'd want.

Maybe this woman was lying to her friend. Maybe working in the store all day was her false alibi. But if so, it wasn't a very good one. If she'd had someone take over for her, even for an hour, someone—one of the other merchants in town—would've noticed. And if she'd closed up in the middle of the day, someone would've noticed that, too.

Maybe she was saying one lie to her friend, and she'd tell a different lie to the police. But that didn't make any sense either. The whole point of a false alibi was that it had to be consistent—otherwise the police would eventually find you out.

I had a bad feeling that coming here had been a mistake, that this woman hadn't been involved in Gilbert's kidnapping.

Then, from somewhere out beyond the walls of the apartment, Emory screamed.

11

Emory's scream sounded like he was right next to me. Maybe he *was*—in the astral dimension, the walls of the house didn't exist to block the sound.

I soared toward the direction of his voice, through the door of the bedroom.

But he wasn't in the bedroom, which had its curtains drawn and was as black as a forgotten tomb. Where else had Emory said he was going?

The garage.

I kept moving forward, through the back wall, and suddenly I was back out in the dim moonlight. The garage was free-standing, off to one side.

I flew through the nearest of its walls. There was a car inside, something small and square, but the garage was big, so there was plenty of extra space. There was a window here, too, but no curtains, so moonlight filtered in, a spotlight against the gloom.

Emory was standing in the light of that window, facing the other end of the garage, his back to me. He'd stopped screaming, but was frozen, as if staring at something in the far corner. There were several circular objects hanging on the wall next to him, but I couldn't make them out in the dark—two coiled garden hoses maybe.

"What is it?" I asked, even as I felt the vaguest tingle of the chill I'd felt twice before, the one in my soul.

Emory didn't look at me. It was like he couldn't move, couldn't even speak. He just kept staring into the corner.

I floated closer and took a look. The shadows were particularly thick there, and I didn't see anything at first. Then I saw something curved and hanging—another coiled garden hose maybe. And there were two small round objects, almost white, suspended in the middle of the coils.

It wasn't a hose. It was some kind of…creature. It was floating in the corner of the garage, not any bigger than a basketball. And it had tentacles or legs of some kind. It looked like a cross between an octopus and a spider. I knew it was alive, because its legs were slowly curling in on themselves.

It's the thing I saw earlier. The tentacle was real.

Now I stood frozen, hanging in space. Somehow I knew it was definitely in the astral dimension with us, a being without actual substance, but something made up of shadow and darkness, not light like Emory and me. Had this creature followed us from the cabin? Emory had said he'd been drawn to me because he'd heard me making all that noise. Maybe this creature had heard me too, and then followed us back here to Hinder Island. I still didn't know how populated the astral dimension was, but from the look of things so far, it was mostly deserted.

It wasn't moving, so I edged closer to Emory. I could see the thing much more clearly now. It definitely wasn't an actual octopus or spider. For one thing, it had more than eight legs—at least a dozen, maybe more. It floated there, quivering slightly with its legs splayed out.

But it had eyes, looking back at us.

Human eyes.

These were the white objects I'd seen floating in the middle of the shadows. Lidless, they peered out at me from near the top of all that blackness. It was the whites of those eyes that had made me realize it wasn't just a shadow in the first place. But as white as they were, the pupils were as black as the rest of the creature, dark and full of hate.

I don't know how I knew with such certainty that these were human eyes, but I did. You could see the intelligence in them, and the anger.

The chill in my soul deepened, and I wanted to look away, but I couldn't. The creature was such an appalling mixture, so obviously alien and yet also somehow human. I'd never seen anything like it—never even *imagined* anything like it. If being in the astral dimension meant becoming aware that the boundaries of the universe are artificial—that we're all one—did that mean I was part of that creature, and it was part of me? It was bad enough that it even existed.

But then, the very instant the creature made sense to me, it was gone. It didn't vanish—it shot away, like a retreating octopus. Unlike an octopus, it didn't leave a cloud of black ink in its wake, but because the creature was so dark, so black, it did seem to leave a dark spot in my vision even after it was gone.

Celestia Moonglow hadn't said anything about *any* of this.

Neither Emory nor I spoke for a second. It had all happened so fast.

Finally, he said, "Let's get out of here. Now."

I didn't need to be told twice. It was all I could do to get out of the dark confines of that garage.

The moonlight was brighter in the small yard just outside, but it was only a small comfort. We were still surrounded by shadows: dark outlines that stretched out beside the ragged rhododendrons and black pools that had gathered under the Madrona tree in the yard or pickup truck parked in the alley. These were all places where the shadowy spider-octopus creature could be hiding, still watching us. The chill I felt still hadn't gone away—I was starting to think it never would. Maybe this was why I'd felt that chill out at Trumble Point, along with the strange sense that something bad was going to happen: because Gilbert was going to be kidnapped and I was going to encounter this horrible creature.

Instinctively, Emory and I both rose up into the sky, away from the shadows. Something flew by us in the dark, and we both flinched at the sound of muffled flapping. But it was just an owl chasing a bat back in the real world.

"What *was* that back there?" I said to Emory, both of us hovering unsteadily now.

"I don't know," he said. The two of us felt the need to whisper. "I was looking around the garage, and I felt something watching me again. I turned, and there it was." Emory was scared—really scared. The same guy who flew like Superman and had let a car pass right through him without jumping.

At least the chill in my soul was slowly leaching away. But there was a different chill taking its place, a kind of unease that didn't have anything to do with the shadow creature.

"Did you find out anything about Gilbert?" I said. "Before the creature, did you see anything?"

Emory shook his head, even as he shivered in the dark. Like me, he was still feeling the chill. "You?" I shook my head. I told him what she'd said on the phone, how I didn't think she was involved in my brother's kidnapping.

"You should still tell the police. It's still really suspicious that she gave Gilbert candy."

"Yeah," I said, no steadier than before, no less uneasy.

"We should go back," Emory said quietly.

I looked at him. "Back?"

"To the real world. To our bodies." This was the unstated thing I hadn't wanted him to say. The only thing worse than that shadow creature was the thought of losing Gilbert.

Reminded of my little brother, I tried briefly listening for him again—but I still didn't hear anything.

"It wasn't a complete loss," Emory said. "You learned Gilbert really was kidnapped—you even know the kidnappers' first names, and a lot more if that's their lake cabin. The police have to be able to do something with all that."

"They already sent a police car out to the cabin," I said. "They didn't find anything. You said they need probable cause to do anything more. Besides, Conrad and Evelyn are already *gone*. They said they're meeting someone—there can't be much more time."

"You could take a car and go search the cabin yourself."

"It's too late. The ferry's already stopped running for the night." I looked up at him with eager eyes. "But you could!"

"What?" He hadn't expected me to say this.

"You said you only live twenty miles away!" I said. "You can take a car and go break into the cabin, and then you can come back here and tell me what you found!"

Emory held up his hands. "Zach, stop! I can't. I don't have a car—I don't even have a driver's license."

"Then call a friend! Have them come and—"

He interrupted me. "Zach, I *can't!* I just…can't. My parents would never let me leave this late at night. And there's no way to sneak out of the house. Besides, you really can't stay here. That thing down there? Who knows what it might do? Use the silver cord. Let it draw you back to your body."

"But it was my last stick of incense!" I said. If I went back now, that was it; I couldn't come back, ever. If I later thought of something else that I could do from the astral dimension to help Gilbert, I wouldn't be able to do it.

Still, Emory had a point. We didn't know for sure what the shadow creature was capable of, but the hatred in its eyes had been all too real.

I felt like a stone that had been sinking through deep water for a long time and had now finally hit bottom.

I could always come back to the New Age shop. I could knock on the door to the woman's apartment, get her to talk to me and tell me everything she knew about astral projection. She might not want to at first, but I'd have to make her understand. And I could trade her something for the special incense—my bike or my cell phone.

From somewhere nearby, something started grinding. It didn't seem very far away, and at first I thought it was tires on gravel. But it didn't have the weird hollow timbre of sounds in the real world. Whatever this was, it seemed to be coming from within the astral dimension.

"What is that?" I said.

Emory shook his head.

I had to check it out. Sure, maybe it had something to do with that shadow creature—but maybe it had something to do with Gilbert, or would lead me to something that did.

"You should go," I said to Emory. I didn't have to take him with me. I didn't have to risk his life, too.

"What?" he said.

"It's too dangerous here. Just like you said."

"Are *you* going home?"

I thought for a second, debating whether to tell him the truth. Finally, I shook my head. "No." I nodded toward the sound. "Whatever that is, it might have something to do with Gilbert."

Emory set his jaw. Some of his old bravado was back. "Then I'm not going back yet, either." But now there was a bit of hesitation in his voice.

Even so, I nodded. This time he'd said what I'd secretly been hoping he'd say.

12

The source of the grinding noise was…a giant purple pin-wheel.

At least that's what it looked like from where Emory and I were, still floating high up in the sky. It hung there, suspended vertically in mid-air above the lawn of one of the houses that surrounded the town of Hinder.

Whatever this thing was, it was definitely with us on our side of the looking glass. It glowed with a purple light, but it didn't seem to be casting any shadows. And it wasn't dimmed by the astral lens.

Just like a pinwheel, it was slowly rotating.

I had to check it out.

"Wait!" Emory said, even as I had already started angling down. "Keep a look out—and avoid the shadows." Unlike me, he hadn't already forgotten about the shadow creature.

We landed in the open lawn area in front of the house. From there, the purple pinwheel looked like some kind of vortex: an eight-foot whirlpool of energy. It was definitely moving, slowly revolving inward, like a satellite photo of the clouds of a rotating hurricane. As it slowly turned, it made a sound like the millstone of a windmill. The vague ethereal breeze still blew, toward the vortex now, but it was easy to withstand.

"What is it?" I said.

"A gate," Emory said.

"A *what?*"

"A doorway to another dimension."

"How do you know that?" I said.

"There was one just like it on an episode of *Buffy the Vampire Slayer.*"

"We're now getting our information about the astral dimension from a TV show?"

Emory shrugged.

I thought back to *Voyage Beyond the Rainbow*. Once again, Celestia Moonglow hadn't said anything about this—despite the totally misleading blurb on the book jacket that had promised readers they could "travel through space and time, visit distant planets, and even travel to different dimensions."

She hadn't said anything about shadow creatures with human eyes either. The truth is, she made a crappy spirit guide. If Celestia Moonglow really had been to the astral dimension in some form, she hadn't done it like I had.

"This doesn't have anything to do with Gilbert," Emory said. "I think we should leave."

"What's going on?" said a voice from the porch of the little house.

It was the shimmering outline of an old man, fat with sweat-matted hair and rumpled pajamas. He was looking right at us, confused, like he'd wandered from his house in the middle of the night. But he was like Emory and me, clear and bright, definitely with us in the astral realm.

"What am I doing outside?" the old man said to us. His whole body shook and wobbled like a person on ice skates for the first time.

"He's doing astral projection," Emory said to me. "Like us."

"Why is everything so dark?" the man said. He gestured at the vortex. "And what in heaven's name is *that*?"

"Don't you know how you got here?" Emory asked the old man.

"No!" said the man in his pajamas. "I was just—" He pointed back at the house behind him, but was interrupted by the sound of sirens. My first thought was that maybe the sirens had something to do with Gilbert, that maybe they'd found him and were returning him home. But my grandparents lived on the other side of the island, and the ferries had shut down for the night now anyway.

A firetruck, lights flashing and siren blaring, pulled up to the house. Other trucks and cars followed. It was paramedics from the island's mostly volunteer fire department.

"Hurry!" said a new voice from the front porch. "He's in here!" It was an old woman in her nightgown. She'd come outside at the sound of the sirens.

"Brenda?" The old man in his pajamas had turned to face the woman on the porch.

She ignored him. Instead, she clutched fearfully at the folds of her nightgown while paramedics quickly unloaded medical equipment from their trucks—cases and backpacks and a stretcher.

"*Brenda!*" the old man said, but now the paramedics were hustling the stretcher and their equipment toward the house. Brenda turned and led them inside.

Slowly the old man looked back at Emory and me. He was made up of light and energy, not flesh and blood, but his face had seemed to pale anyway.

Unlike Emory and me, the old man didn't have a silver cord. He wasn't attached to his body.

"Does this mean I'm dead?" the old man whispered.

I didn't know what to say. It sure looked that way.

So this is what happened to my parents, I thought.

"Who *are* you?" the man demanded, suddenly angry. "Where *am* I?"

"I'm sorry," Emory said. "We really don't know much more than you do."

"Look, there's been some kind of mistake," the old man said.

"I'm sorry, but we—"

"I need to get back inside!" The old man was panicking. When he tried to walk, he just flailed, skating now on cracking ice. He didn't understand how to move in the astral dimension.

The vortex ground louder, like the rumble of distant thunder. It was moving more quickly now, roiling, like water beginning to circle down a drain.

"What *is* that?" said the old man. "What's happening?"

"Zach," Emory said. "Get back."

Together we floated backward, away from the vortex.

"Wait!" said the old man. "Where are you going? What's *happening*?"

Something exploded in the middle of the vortex. I thought I saw purple flames. The swirling continued to pick up speed. The hair and clothes of the old man began to flutter, pulled in the direction of the whirlpool, like the breeze was now trying to draw him inside.

"Get back!" I said to the man. "Get away from the gate."

But the old man was barely moving. He was still trying to walk, even as the draw of the vortex grew stronger. He floundered, searching for something to hold onto, but when he reached the railing on the porch, his fingers passed right through it.

The old man slid awkwardly back toward the whirl-pool. It was spinning much faster now. The rumble sounded like a low growl.

"Help me!" said the man. "It's pulling me in!"

"You have to use your mind," Emory said. "That's how you stop yourself."

But he didn't have any idea how mind power worked. He'd just arrived here.

"We have to help him," Emory said.

I nodded.

Emory drifted tentatively toward the old man. "Hold me," he said to me. I reached forward and placed my hands on his waist. I felt the same connection that I'd felt before, the same tingle of electricity, and I was embarrassed that I was thinking about the feel of his body at a time like this.

Once I had a good grip on him, we floated closer to the vortex together. Our own clothes and hair fluttered. We were clearly just as susceptible to the suction as the old man.

"Take my hand!" Emory said to him, reaching for his outstretched fingers.

"I can't reach!" the man said. "Come closer!"

We levitated closer to the man in the pajamas, even as he slid backward, closer to the vortex. He was now less than five feet away from its swirling center.

"Hold onto my ankles," Emory said to me.

"Emory—" I started to say.

"Do it!"

I crouched and gripped his ankles with both hands. Emory let himself fall forward, surrendering to the suction of the vortex. The pull held him aloft and allowed him to reach the old man. Their hands met, his fingers closing around the man's.

"Now!" Emory said to me. "Pull us back!"

I slipped Emory's ankles under my armpits, gripping him around the shins, and *willed* myself back away from this strange astral cyclone.

Slowly we all started moving away.

The vortex exploded again, now spinning faster still. Purple flames definitely shot from its center, and the growl became an impatient roar. Emory's and my mind power weren't the only forces at work here.

Before I knew it, we'd been dragged right back to the place where we'd started.

"Zach?" Emory said.

"I'm trying," I said. "I'm *trying*." My struggle was mental, but I felt it in my entire astral body.

I squeezed Emory's legs more tightly. But no matter how hard I tried to will myself backward, we weren't moving. The suction from the vortex was too strong—and growing stronger.

The old man screamed. I could feel him squirming at the far end of Emory's body.

"Help me!" he said. "It's pulling me in!"

His feet disappeared into the center of the vortex. Emory still had him by the hand, but both he and the man were now completely horizontal against the vortex.

My feet slipped. Not only could I not move them away from the vortex, but now it was pulling us all in.

"Zach!" Emory said.

"I know!" I said. "It's too strong. It's pulling us in."

"Don't let go!" said the old man. "Don't let me go!" By now, he was buried in the vortex up to his thighs, sinking like a man caught in quicksand.

Emory's hand was less than six feet from the center of the maelstrom.

My feet slid again. More than ever, it was like the whole dimension was made of grease. If Emory didn't let him go soon, the old man would pull them both in.

"Emory!" I said.

"I'm sorry," Emory said to the man. "I can't hold on!"

The old man's eyes bulged. "No! *Please!*"

"Hey!" Emory said, and I felt him struggling in the old man's arms. Emory glanced back at me. "He won't let go."

The old man was now holding Emory's hand, not the other way around.

"Let him go!" I said to the man. "You'll pull us all in!"

"No!" the old man said. "*Don't let me go!*"

The old man slipped deeper inside, like a rat being swallowed by a snake. But no matter how Emory tugged and pulled at the old man's hand, he wouldn't let Emory go.

"Zach?" Emory said, panicking at last.

"I've got you," I said. "I'm not letting you go."

The old man screamed again, a horrible wail. He was now just a head and an arm—and a hand that still had an impossibly tight grip on Emory.

The scream stopped in mid-shriek. The vortex had claimed his head. But even now, he somehow still had a hold on Emory.

"*Zach*." Now he was on the verge of screaming, too.

"I've *got* you," I said. But no matter how hard I fought to stop us, we kept inching closer to the maelstrom.

The old man was now gone completely. One part of me was certain that the cyclone would stop pulling us in now that it had taken him.

But the sucking didn't stop. The pinwheel just kept spinning, its roar louder than ever. Emory's hand dipped into the vortex.

"Zach!" Emory said. "He's still got me. He still won't let go."

"I'm not letting go either," I said.

Soon Emory was up to his elbow.

Then his shoulder.

"Zach!" he said. "Let me go!"

"No!" I said.

"Let me go and save yourself. Get away from here!"

"No!" I repeated.

"Don't be stupid! Let me—" His head had dipped into the vortex, silencing him.

I still had his feet, and I was *determined* to get him back out again.

Emory started kicking in my arms, just as determined to get me to let him go.

"Stop!" I shouted, but he didn't hear me. I still didn't let go.

His shoulders followed his head into the vortex.

The rest of his body began slowly to disappear, like a cucumber into a vegetable chopper.

"*NO!*" I screamed.

I told myself that the vortex wouldn't claim one more inch of his body.

Then, without warning, he came away in my arms.

13

It was like I'd been playing a game of tug-of-war and the other side had just given up. I fell back from the vortex, pulling Emory with me. Thankfully his astral body was all intact.

I was all set to pull him even farther away, but the second we were free, the cyclone began one long, final swirl, sucking in on itself.

And then it was gone. The vortex had disappeared.

Still a little stunned, Emory and I stared at the space where the vortex had been. The glow was gone, so darkness had reclaimed the yard. There wasn't even a wisp of astral smoke as evidence that there had been anything there at all. The grinding of the vortex was gone now, too, and the relative silence, the mere moan of the astral dimension, was strange.

"What happened?" I said.

"I don't know," Emory said. "He finally let me go."

"Where were you? What did you see?"

"Nothing. It was too dark. For the record, I could hear the old man screaming. Then I felt a hard jerk on his body. Like something…grabbed him. Then he let go."

I was still holding onto Emory's astral body—I still had my arms wrapped tightly around his legs. I could feel the same electrical connection I'd felt before, only it was stronger now with more of our bodies touching. Our silver cords had also somehow become entwined, at least for a few feet, and it seemed like I could feel that, too. The touch of Emory's cord against mine felt like someone stroking my hair.

"Thank God you're okay," I said.

"Thanks to you," he said.

"What?"

He pulled away and levitated upright. Our astral bodies weren't touching anymore, but our cords were, so it felt like we were still connected.

"You didn't let go of me," he said. "Even when it looked like I was going to pull you in."

"You tried to save me, too," I said. "You tried to get me to let go of you." His brown eyes were warm and open—the opposite of that creature in the garage in every way. But they were also now openly sad.

Emory looked away as he let himself drift farther from me. I was surprised how easily our astral cords separated. Either they hadn't been as entwined as I'd thought, or they'd passed right through each other.

"Gilbert," he said.

"What about him?" Instinctively, I listened again, but I still couldn't hear him.

"You should see if he's back."

I didn't want to go back to my body now. It sounds strange given all that had happened in the last few minutes—seeing that creature in the garage and then almost being sucked into some alien dimension. Something about Emory's touch had grounded me—made me less afraid. Besides, the shadow creature had *looked* scary, but it had also darted away as soon as it had seen us. Maybe it was even more afraid of us than we were of it, like monsters always are in children's books.

"Let's go together," I said. "My grandparents' house isn't that far from here."

———

It seemed like a bad sign that there was no police car parked outside the house. The police wouldn't bring Gilbert home, drop him off, and immediately leave again. Then again, the ferries had stopped running for the night.

They could've found Gilbert and kept him on the other side of the water, waiting until morning to return him.

Emory and I sank down through the roof.

I hadn't intended to pass through my room, but we did. The light on the nightstand was still on, and I saw my body lying in bed.

It was fully dressed and completely motionless. My breathing was so shallow that I had to stare in order to see it. It was hard not to be reminded of a corpse.

I'd been in the astral dimension so long now that I'd kind of started to think of it as normal. This was a reminder of just how much it wasn't.

Emory followed me through the wall to Gilbert's room. The lights were off, and for a moment, I thought I saw someone sleeping in his bed. But it was just lumps in the comforter.

I led Emory down to the kitchen where my grandparents were still waiting by the phone. I expected them to be pacing anxiously, but they were both motionless again, sitting at the kitchen table, cups of coffee, probably stone cold, in mugs in front of them. As long as I'd known them, my grandparents had never looked young. But they both looked positively ancient now, so old that they didn't even look human—more like mummies propped upright, brittle and unmoving.

"I'll find him," I said to them softly. "I will."

But they didn't look up, didn't even know I was there.

As I was watching my grandparents, I sensed Emory watching me.

"Zach," he said at last. "I need to tell you something."

I turned his way.

"It's the real reason I'm here in the astral dimension," he said. "I don't have any of the special incense that you use. I don't need it. I just need to meditate. For the record, I have been here before, quite a few times."

"Really? That's great." I confess I was a little jealous. "Have you, like, seen the whole world? Have you been to other planets? Could we travel to Jupiter?"

"I've never thought about going to another planet. And I haven't seen the whole world. But I've seen those gates before. That's how I knew what they were, not *Buffy the Vampire Slayer*."

"What about other people? Have you run into any of those?"

He thought for a second. "The weird thing is, in all the time I've been coming here, you're the only other person I've ever seen."

I wondered what this meant—if the woman in the New Age shop had been right and people like Celestia Moonglow weren't really coming here at all, but were just dreaming or imagining the whole thing. And yet Emory had been able to do it for real, without the incense.

"How long did it take you to get this good?" I said.

"My whole life," he said.

I looked at him, confused.

"I'm paraplegic." He said this last part without any warning, so I hadn't expected it, didn't know what to make of it.

I looked down at his legs, at his whole body hanging solidly in the middle of my grandparents' kitchen.

"Not here," he said. "Back in the real world. I use a wheelchair."

I thought about this. It did explain a few things: not just Emory's exaggerated movements in the astral dimension, but his bravado and the vulnerability it masked. And this must've been why he hadn't been willing to drive back to the cabin on Silver Lake for me; maybe he couldn't drive.

"It happened was when I was a kid," he said. "Viral infection. I'm paralyzed from the waist down."

I thought about what he was saying, tried to make sense of it, even as I waited for my own emotional reaction. It unfolded like a paper snowflake in my mind, slowly, and even I was curious to see the end result.

"My parents don't understand...anything," he said. "They're really religious. They control everything: what I read, what I watch, what friends I see. If I were anyone else, I think people would think it's strange how controlling they are—even relatives of ours. But with a paraplegic kid, people think it's normal, that I'm helpless, that my parents *should* control everything about my life. For the record, my parents sometimes let me go the library, and I read about astral projection in this book, years ago. I really wanted to come here. It sounded like a place where I could be...free."

Like I'd been drawn to the Internet because I was trapped on an island. Emory and I weren't so different at all.

"So I started meditating," he went on. "It didn't work for a long time—so long that I didn't even really remember why I'd started meditating in the first place. But about two months ago, I finally did it."

I thought about everything he'd said. "None of this changes anything," I said at last. "But why didn't you tell me before?"

He scoffed. "Like anyone would be interested in a boyfriend who can't walk."

A boyfriend. So Emory and I were alike in more ways than one. Was that what he thought we might become—boyfriends?

I glanced nervously over at my grandparents sitting at the kitchen table, but they still hadn't moved. They didn't even know we were there.

"It makes no difference to me," I said to Emory. This was the absolute truth. "You could've told me before."

"When?" he said. "We were so caught up in looking for your brother."

My brother.

"But mostly I think I was ashamed," he went on. "Not that I'm paraplegic—I'm not ashamed about that. It's that when I ended up in the astral dimension, I turned up without my wheelchair."

I didn't understand.

Emory saw the confusion in my eyes. "This is how we see ourselves." He gestured at his body, lean and athletic. "I mean, these clothes don't really exist, right? It's all some kind of illusion from our minds, some projection of our ideal self—it has to be. But my ideal self...can walk. There's no wheelchair! What does that say about me, about the way I see myself? I feel like such a traitor to the cause. That probably sounds funny to you, and maybe you can't understand. But us gimps—people in wheelchairs—we're not supposed to think of ourselves as broken, you know? And it makes sense. I mean, who wants to go through life like that, feeling like they're fundamentally flawed? And I don't, I really don't. Except maybe some part of me does, because I like it here. I like feeling whole again. And that makes me feel guilty."

With all that had happened in the last day, Gilbert missing and meeting Emory and now learning all this about him, I couldn't remember my heart ever being open so wide, so full of both love and pain, not even when my parents died.

"Emory," I said. "You don't have anything to feel bad about." I searched for the words. I wanted to tell him I understood, that I could relate, even if I probably couldn't, not really. "We both had our reasons for coming here. Maybe they weren't always the purest of reasons, but we are who we are. We don't have anything to apologize for. I'm just glad we—"

In the middle of my sentence, the shadow creature with the tentacle-like legs leapt out at me—from the spot in the real world where the refrigerator was—and landed right on top of my head.

14

It all happened so fast.

I saw movement coming at me from one side, but before I could move, the shadow creature had wrapped itself around my head like a hood. Before I could even think, the thing's finger-like tentacles were stuck to my face.

It wasn't like a monster in some children's book; it wasn't more afraid of us than we were of it.

I stiffened in surprise. It had covered my eyes, and even though I wasn't necessarily "seeing" through them in the astral dimension, I suddenly couldn't see at all. Still, I could definitely *feel* the creature. It was everything I'd felt that afternoon out at Trumble Point—that terrible *chill*, the deep sense of menace—and more. It was the opposite of Emory's touch. Rather than that gentle, electric connection, I felt its cold, heavy presence bearing down on me, overpowering me. I felt no mouth—it was like the whole creature was a mouth, opening to consume me. And yet, somehow I also knew that it didn't want to merely eat me. It wanted to destroy me, to replace me, to somehow *become* me.

It was all too much. One second I'd been slowly drifting on the ethereal breeze across my grandparents' kitchen, having a heart-to-heart with Emory. The next second I'd been attacked, and my soul was about to be swallowed by some vile shadow creature. I could hear Emory's muffled screams from outside my helmet of shadows, but I couldn't make out what he was saying.

I had to fight back. Even now, I sensed a change in the thing, a gathering of purpose. It was shifting even as it clutched my head, starting some kind of weird metamorphosis. I couldn't see its eyes, those dark, hateful things I'd seen in the garage, but I could somehow *feel* them—above me, looking down *at* me, greedy and determined, boring into me. But at the same time, I couldn't move—like I'd somehow been drugged or anesthetized. I wanted to fight back, but I couldn't. My mind wanted something, but my astral body wouldn't or couldn't react. How was that possible in a place where my mind *was* my body? Maybe I didn't want it after all. As I floated there, the will to fight back was dripping off me like sap down the trunk of a pierced maple. After a second, I didn't even feel the cold chill in my soul anymore.

"Get off me," I said to the thing on my head, but it was half-hearted at best. I wasn't sure I had actually even spoken the words.

I reached limply up and tried to grab the thing. It was elusive—trying to touch it was like trying to grab a cloud of smoke. In the end, though, there was definitely something there. It was squishy and slick, like an oily cushion.

It was clutching my head like a starfish about to feast on the tender innards of a clam. There was no way I was going to tear it off, not as tired as I felt.

But as my astral hands fumbled for this evil, alien thing, I happened to brush something unexpected—something small and orb-like near the top of its head. It was much more solid than the rest of its body, hard, like a large marble.

I'd touched one of its eyes. Ironically, while the rest of its body was soft, its eyes were hard—the opposite of a human body. Its eyes had somehow migrated to the top of its head.

But it hadn't expected me to touch its eye, and doing so meant that I somehow had access to its mind. It was as if, in preparing to invade my mind, the creature had accidentally left its own psyche wide open. And so, just by touching one of its eyes, I found myself slipping deep into the recesses of its mind.

It all happened in an instant—my touch and a resulting flood of what seemed like…memories. As I glimpsed these memories, it was like I transported back into the past—someone else's past—experiencing it as if for the first time.

————

I am missing a heart. There are only four of them on the bloody table in front of me. How is that possible? Why is it so easy to lose things in this basement? Then again, I did buy the place for the extra space, not to mention the privacy. "Like a dungeon," the real estate agent had said. If only she knew.

No matter, I think. The missing organ is bound to turn up eventually. In the meantime, there's still more work to do.

I turn to the man chained to the basement's far wall. "This may hurt a little," I say, but I know he can't hear me over the sound of the chainsaw.

————

I wasn't disgusted by the memory—not yet anyway—because I was the one experiencing it, not just witnessing it. But at the same time, the part of me that was still me thought, *Why does the shadow creature have human memories? And why the memories of some kind of mass murderer?*

But even as I thought that, I touched a different, deeper memory inside the mind of the shadow-being, and was suddenly transported to an earlier place and time.

I stare at the carnage in the bedroom in front of me. The mattress is a giant sponge; it's almost completely soaked with blood. I'm reminded again how much of the stuff there is inside the human body. I look down at the bloodless corpses lying atop the bed. It's always very unsatisfying when my victims don't struggle, and these two barely let out a scream. They put up far too brave a face.

Perhaps I'll have better luck with their children, tied up in the chair next to the bed, especially now that they've seen what I've done to their parents.

———

These were different men, the one who was separating body parts in his basement, and the one who was torturing and killing that family—I knew that for a fact. I just wasn't sure how the mind of the shadow creature could hold the memories of two different people. Maybe the creature had eaten the souls of both these men and somehow collected both their memories inside itself. If so, both had gotten what they deserved.

Or *were* these two different people? They'd inhabited different bodies, but somehow they *felt* the same, as if the shadow creature had lived more than one life. How was *that* possible?

I'd seen enough. I hadn't intended to touch the eyes or the mind of this creature in the first place. I'd said before that if being one with the universe meant being connected to this creature, I didn't want any of part of it, and here I was, connected to it in a more personal, intimate way than I'd ever thought possible. I had literally *become* it.

I tried to pull my hand away, but I was in too deep. More lives passed before me, each somehow seen from the same set of eyes. I couldn't stop the memories from coming, one after the other, each one older than the last.

———

I am determined to ignore the pipe organ of the Ferris wheel outside my office window. Then someone screams in the room behind me, and all thoughts of the Ferris wheel are forgotten. My latest victim has finally woken up. I smile as she begins to shriek in panic, as if she somehow instinctively knows that the vault is airtight and she will soon suffocate. Alas, then I'll have to deal with the sound of that insufferable Ferris wheel again.

———

I stare at the huddle of dark-skinned bodies in the bottom of the pit. They're clinging to each other in the mud. "Now shoot them all," I say to the soldiers at my side, and the sergeant pretends to be shocked by his general's orders. But the lieuten-

ant isn't shocked; he's been waiting eagerly for this. The first of the shots ring out. There are those who say that it makes more sense to kill the Indian braves first, so they can't fight back, but I know better; kill the women and children, and the braves have nothing left to fight for.

———

It's mid-October, and an early winter has descended on the forest, but I don't fear the cold. I have the makings of a campfire to keep me warm this night, and a new cache of supplies to see me through the hard months ahead. I light the kindling, and pitch begins to snap and pop in the flames. It lights as quickly as I thought it would, and soon a conflagration illuminates the night. It warms me, but not as much as the screams of the old fool I had tied to the stake in the middle of the blaze.

———

I managed to stop the flood of memories at last. I hadn't been disgusted by the memories while I had been experiencing them, but now that I'd stopped them, now that I had some distance, I was a feeling of revulsion washed over me like a cold mist. My grandparents had always been worried about evil in the world, about all the bad things that happened over on the mainland—and *only* there, they thought. But they had no *idea* just how evil people could be, what bad things did happen in the world—even on islands, unfortunately.

I hadn't had any idea either.

And while it was bad enough that I'd had to watch them, I'd also been forced to experience them, to actually be the one who did these terrible things without remorse. It was a different kind of horror, so ghastly that it had even managed to penetrate the dullness that the creature had somehow created in my brain.

"What *are* you?" I shouted at the shadow creature in my hands.

Suddenly another vision, the earliest memory in a long stream of them, flashed before my eyes. Now I did know exactly what—or, rather, *who*—the being was, and exactly what it wanted.

The creature chose this moment to fight back.

First, despite having no lids, it somehow closed its eyes. In that instant, I was locked out of its mind.

Then the creature wiggled forward, to the back of my head, out of my awkward, exhausted reach. Once again, the tentacle-like legs gripped me, and its body began to metamorphose again—into what, I wasn't sure, but it was clearly intent on consuming the soul it had been so close to winning before.

At least I could see again.

But this time, I had no defenses. This time, I was just too tired, overwhelmed by the creature's anesthesia and by what I had seen in its mind. I couldn't even raise a finger against it. My mind reeled. Since the start of its attack, the whole encounter had only been a couple of seconds.

I felt the creature quiver in anticipation.

And I saw Emory reach out and grab the creature with both hands. Somehow he twisted it from the top of my head and threw it roughly to one side. *It looks so black*, I thought dully as the creature flew, undulating, into the shadows. *Like a void, like a blind spot moving across my vision.*

But at least it was gone—for the moment at least. Already my sense of self was coming back to me.

Emory didn't wait for it to attack again. Instead he grabbed me and pulled me with him up through the darkened rooms of my grandparents' house, high into the sky. When we were a couple hundred feet up, Emory released me and let me float free as he stared down into the shadows below, a night watchman on the highest of alert. For a second I thought I was going to plunge right back to the ground, but somehow I steadied myself.

"The thing," he said, watching me carefully. "What was it doing? Why was it after you?"

"It wasn't after me, at least not at first," I said. I had so much to tell him, but I didn't know where to begin. "It was after you."

15

Emory stared at me as I swayed back and forth in the air like some kind of drunken high wire act. I was beyond shaken. What made Emory think we were safe from that creature just because we'd flown up into the sky?

"Thanks," I said quietly.

"For what?" Emory said.

"Saving my life."

"Just returning the favor. But what did you mean about the creature? It's trying to kill me?"

"It doesn't want to kill either of us. Not exactly." I thought for a second, trying to figure out how to put into words everything I'd learned. "It's trying to *possess* us. It wants to take control of our souls to return to the physical world."

"How do you—"

"As it attacked me, I somehow touched its mind. It was human once."

"That thing was human?"

"A long time ago."

"And you touched its *mind?*" As we talked, Emory stared down into the darkness. But if the creature came upon us again, would we even be able to see it in the night? It was so *black*.

I started to explain what I'd learned, beginning with the last thing I had seen in its mind, the deepest memory. "It was human," I said. "But that was hundreds of years ago."

"Hundreds of—" Emory said.

"Just listen. His name was Alistair Thorn. He was born in western Pennsylvania. But from a really young age, he liked to kill things. People sensed he was different, even his parents, so he left home at a young age—he knew he wouldn't be missed, and he wasn't. Soon he discovered that the thing he loved to kill more than anything was people. But that was hard to do in the settled areas of Pennsylvania. So he left for the frontier.

"But the people he met on the frontier weren't easy victims. They were well-armed and suspicious, even harder to kill than the people back in Pennsylvania. Alistair wouldn't have survived at all if he hadn't found this Indian shaman named Bitter Eye. He had been thrown out of his tribe for practicing dark magic.

"Alistair and Bitter Eye traveled together for months. At first Alistair laughed at the shaman's weird fireside prayers. But Bitter Eye's powers seemed real—he somehow saw things that turned out to be true—so Alistair talked the Indian into sharing what he knew. Bitter Eye taught Alistair how to enter the spirit world—the astral dimension.

"Alistair was evil, but he wasn't stupid. He was a fast learner and had a strong mind. Bitter Eye saw how powerful he was growing, but he was also starting to see just how evil Alistair was. So he betrayed him to a group of Indians who ended up killing him. But Alistair was able to use what he'd learned about astral travel to cheat death."

This part was complicated, and I was so tired that talking felt like rolling a boulder up a hill. But it was important that Emory understand.

"That vortex?" I said to Emory. "You were right. It's a gateway that opened up in order to take that old man's spirit to a different dimension. But when Alistair's physical body was killed by those Indians, his spirit didn't die. A gate opened up for him, just like it opened for that old man. But by now Alistair was so comfortable in the astral dimension, and so mentally strong, that he was able to *avoid* the gate. His body died, but his spirit lived on inside the astral dimension. But over the centuries, the astral dimension has changed him. His spirit has become less and less human. Or like you said, maybe that's just how he sees himself now.

"And even here in the astral dimension, he was driven to kill. So he started attacking the spirits of the other humans he came across. Some of them were strong enough to fight him off. But some of them weren't—the spirits of the dead were almost always weak and confused, and even some of the spirits of the living were, too. And if these living spirits were weak enough, he discovered he could do more than just kill them. He could *possess* them."

If these living spirits were weak enough, I thought.

"Living humans hardly ever come fully into the astral realm," I said. "It's way too hard for most people. But every now and then, one does. Alistair found if he could possess these spirits, he could follow the silver cord back to their body. Then he could possess that body, too. In other words, he was able to go back to the real world and be a human again, and live the rest of that body's life. Sort of a very warped form of reincarnation.

"And once back in the real world, he kept on killing— starting with Bitter Eye himself. But it was even worse this time. The one thing that keeps most serial killers in check is the idea that they might get caught, that they might never be able to kill again. Alistair didn't have to worry about that now. If he got caught, he knew he could just move on to another body. So his kills got more and more complicated. And this is exactly what he's done, again and again, for hundreds of years now."

Down below us, something rustled in the shadows— maybe it was the shadow creature, or maybe it was just an animal in the real world.

"But what does all this have to do with me?" Emory said.

The astral breeze had changed directions, blowing us back toward the interior of the island. Or maybe we were caught in a different current entirely. Didn't the astral realm ever just *stop?*

"At first I thought it was me who had drawn the creature to us," I said. "You heard me when I was making all that noise out at the cottage on Silver Lake, so I figured maybe the same thing that drew your attention had also attracted it. But at that point, it was already stalking you. That's why you were the first to sense it—because it's been following you. It started tracking you over a week ago—it's seen you in the astral dimension three times before. It's just been waiting for the right opportunity to overpower you."

"Because it thinks I'm weak," Emory said.

"Not as weak as it thinks I am," I said. "It knows I took some kind of a shortcut to get here, that I didn't have the mental discipline to come here on my own. Now it's mostly after me. It attacked me in my grandparents' kitchen because I was distracted, so focused on you."

"So what are you saying?" Emory said. "If I'd kept coming here and we hadn't met, the creature would've eventually overpowered me?"

"It would've tried. But it was waiting for just the right moment because it knows that when it attacks and fails, the person usually doesn't ever come back to the astral dimension again."

Emory laughed a bitter laugh. "It would've been in for a real surprise when it got back to my body."

"It knew about your body," I said. "It didn't care. It's more excited by how young you are—how young *we* are." I wasn't telling Emory the whole truth, here. Part of the reason the creature wanted me more now was because of my body, the fact I could walk.

Emory just stared at me.

"We need to go home now," I said. "Back to our bodies. And we can't ever come back."

"But Zach—"

"There's no but. There's too much we don't understand about this place."

There was one other thing I wasn't telling Emory: the shadow creature wasn't the only being of its kind in the astral dimension. Over the centuries, it had come across other creatures like itself—some human, some not. That afternoon at Trumble Point, I must've felt the chill of one of them. Humans could sometimes feel such astral evils all the way over in the material world. It might have even been this shadow creature that I'd touched that day, although it didn't seem to have any memory of me.

"What about Gilbert?" Emory said.

Gilbert, I thought. Out of the corner of my eye, I saw my silver cord buckle and writhe.

"The creature thinks we're weak, but it still needs us to be distracted in order to take possession of us, right?" Emory said. "It needs certain…conditions."

"I…I'm not sure," I said. Nothing was crystal clear. My glimpse into its mind had happened so fast.

"It must. Otherwise it would've attacked me the first time it saw me here."

Emory had kind of a point, but the fact was, the creature hadn't attacked him right away because it had sensed he was stronger mentally, more prepared for the astral dimension. It knew I wasn't.

"We can still look for Gilbert," he said. "We can go to the airports and marinas. It's a long shot, but at least it's a shot."

I thought about all this. It was tempting, but then I remembered the blood.

"You don't understand," I said. "You didn't see what I saw, how evil it is, the things it's done. It *can't* get control of our bodies. The police can still find Gilbert. I know the kidnappers' names, like you said. I'll just have to find a way to make the police understand that."

But there was no point in going to visit the woman from the New Age shop. I had no interest in coming back to the astral dimension ever again.

"We won't be able to see each other," Emory said softly. "I wasn't kidding when I said my parents won't allow that."

I'd forgotten about this. Emory's parents wouldn't let us meet in person, and he had almost no access to the Internet. Which meant this relationship was over before it had even begun.

"That makes me really sad," I said. "But there's no other way."

Emory nodded. This time it was his silver cord that tensed.

"Goodbye," he said. The night reflected in his eyes grew darker still.

"Goodbye," I said. Looking down, I saw that the breeze had already blown us hundreds of feet from my grandparents' house.

I leaned back, trying to relax, ready to let my silver cord pull me back home. Emory did the same.

At that very moment, I heard the sound of a little boy crying.

16

"Emory!" I said. "Wait!"

"Huh?" Like me, he'd been on the verge of slipping away, back to his physical body across the water.

"It's Gilbert!" I said. "I can hear him again." I hadn't even been listening, but I could suddenly hear him loud and clear. It was different than before, not the sniffle I'd first heard or the outright bawling out at the cabin, but a slight whimpering—the sound of a boy who had been crying for a long time with no hope in sight.

Emory listened for a second. "Wait. I hear it, too."

This was strange. It contradicted what we'd said before, that you had to know a person well before you were able to focus on them from the astral dimension.

I listened more closely. It definitely sounded different, but I couldn't quite put my finger on how.

"It sounds like it's coming from nearby," Emory said. "Like it's coming from your grandparents' house."

So this wasn't the sound of Gilbert resounding across the astral dimension. Is that why Emory could hear him—because he was nearby? But Gilbert had been taken off-island hours ago, and the ferries were no longer running. He couldn't be back yet.

Unless the police brought him back in a boat. This was a perfectly logical explanation.

"Something isn't right," Emory said. "He sounds upset. If the police found him and brought him home, would he sound upset?"

"Let's find out," I said, already turning and heading back toward the house.

"But Zach!" he called after me. "What about the creature?"

"What *about* it?" I said, annoyed. I'd said everything I said before when I'd thought finding Gilbert was a complete long shot—not when it sounded like he was crying 100 feet away.

"It's still down there," Emory said. "It can still attack us. Or what if it's the one making those sounds? Maybe this is a trap."

I hadn't thought about this. I knew for a fact that the creature wanted me, and that it was smart.

"Listen to it," I said, meaning the cry. "It's got that echo. It's not coming from the astral dimension. It's coming from the real world."

The whimpering faded away.

"It's stopping!" I said. If Gilbert wasn't home and safe, if Gilbert hadn't been found by the police, there'd be no way to investigate this sound if I went back to my body now. And maybe Emory was right about the creature not attacking unless the conditions were absolutely perfect. If I stayed vigilant, I wouldn't be giving it an opportunity to strike.

The crying started again.

"You go home," I said to Emory. "I just need to check this out, but I'll be really, really careful."

"You know I'm not leaving you alone," he said as he followed me down.

———

The sound wasn't coming from my grandparents' house. It was coming from the house across the street—Billy's place. I couldn't figure out why Gilbert would be over there.

There was a blond boy sitting, sniffling, on the porch swing of Billy's mom's house.

"Gilbert!" I said, zooming toward my brother.

But halfway there, I slowed.

It wasn't Gilbert—it was Billy. He was up late into the night, waiting for some news about his kidnapped best friend. He was the one who had been crying.

As this realization sunk in, I slowed to a stop. I hung limply in the air.

Emory came up behind me. "Zach?"

"It's the wrong kid," I said. "It's his friend Billy. I mistook him for Gilbert. It wasn't Gilbert we heard."

Emory didn't say anything, just reached over and took my hand. The electrical touch was back, but I barely noticed. I was too disappointed by what had happened.

Up on the porch of the house, the front door opened, and Billy's mother joined him on the porch.

"How ya doin'?" she asked him quietly.

The porch swing squeaked. "Okay," Billy said.

Billy's mother sat down next to him on the swing. "They'll find him. He'll be just fine. You wait and see."

"But what if they don't?"

"They will. I promise."

Billy fell silent. The promise of Billy's mom was the kind of thing parents always say to kids—basically, a worthless lie.

"It's not Gilbert," I said. Then, to no one in particular, I shouted, "*It's not Gilbert!*" But voices didn't echo in the astral dimension, even at night. There was nothing to echo against.

"Zach," Emory said. "Don't …"

I immediately felt stupid. Here I'd said I was going to be so careful, and what's the first thing I do? Shriek into the ether, probably attracting the attention of the shadow creature—not to mention all the other astral nasties that might be lurking in the shadows around us.

But I was suddenly consumed with rage. We still weren't any closer to finding Gilbert! It was funny that Emory saw the astral dimension as a place of freedom and possibility. For me, it had been like Hinder Island: nothing but dead ends.

Before Emory could say another word, or tell me we needed to get out of the shadows, I leapt up into the sky. I cleared the treetops in seconds, but was still so angry—at my own stupidity, and at my powerlessness in the face of everything that had happened.

So I didn't stop. I just kept rising, higher and faster into the night. It was as if I thought I could *outrun* my anger, leave it in the air below me. Or maybe I just wanted to *do* something—anything!—since helping Gilbert was apparently out of the question.

"Zach!" Emory called from underneath me, following after.

I ignored him, just kept barreling higher into the sky. I wasn't screaming, or making any noise at all. I put all the emotion into my furious upward flight.

I wasn't sure how long I flew like that, but when I finally stopped and looked around, I was confused. For a second, the vast dark dome below me didn't make any sense.

It was the *Earth* I was seeing rising up underneath me. I had actually cleared the atmosphere. It was mostly dark on the side of the planet below, the side of night. I could still make out the continents, North and South America, but only because of the glowing pinpricks of light from the cities, mostly along the edges of the land. I wasn't in orbit around the Earth exactly, because I still had no physical presence and wasn't affected by gravity. But I was moving across the heavens, probably on the ethereal breeze, or maybe I was just seeing the turning of the Earth below me.

Even after all I'd experienced, it was almost too much to take in. I wasn't scared. I knew I didn't need to breathe, that I was protected from the radiation of the sun and the vacuum of space. I looked at my silver cord spiraling down underneath me, thinner than I'd ever seen it, like twine. It looked like the smoky trail to a skyrocket, but frozen, as if in some photograph, yet to explode. I now knew they could stretch pretty far without breaking—maybe it could stretch forever.

A second later, another form materialized nearby. Emory hung, suspended in the ether opposite me, not fifteen feet away.

I watched the confusion on his face turn to wonder as he, too, realized where we were.

Finally he looked over at me and smiled. "Feel better?"

"No," I said. But the truth was I did feel better. It's not that I'd left my emotions behind. It's just that looking down at the vast expanse of the Earth at night, it was impossible not to put them into perspective, to have a handle on them again. My anger was gone at last. If I had been a skyrocket, I wouldn't have wanted to explode— I would've wanted to keep burning. It even felt like I'd finally left the oppressive shadows of the astral dimension behind. Sure, most of the surface of the Earth was dark, and we were surrounded by the great, glittering void of space. But those shadows were suddenly so far away from us. It was as if, here in the heavens above the Earth, all individual shadows had been banished.

"Emory, what am I going to do?" I asked him. Here I was, suspended high above the Earth at night—probably one of the most astounding sights I would ever see—but all I could think about was Gilbert.

"We'll keep looking if you want," Emory said. "We'll keep listening. And sooner or later, we'll find him again."

To my surprise, our voices didn't sound small in the infinity of the heavens. On the contrary, we'd never sounded so clear.

"You know how they say that an only child is supposed to be so independent, so self-sufficient?" I said.

Emory nodded.

"That wasn't true for me," I said. "I remember when I was a boy, before Gilbert was born, I was afraid of everything. I guess when I was five and had to go to kindergarten, I bawled for a week. But with most kids when their parents tell that story, it ends with the parents saying, 'But then he stopped crying and he had the time of his life!'

I didn't. I mean, it got better, I guess. But *I* didn't really change, not until Gilbert was born.

"I remember the day my parents brought him home. I looked at him, and I felt this connection, you know? Like he was somehow a part of me, like I wasn't alone in the world any more. It's not like I was never lonely after that. I was. But I never felt *completely* alone.

"And then when our parents died? I tell myself that it's my Internet friends that kept me sane, but that's not really true. It was Gilbert. It wasn't anything he said or did. It's that he was there. And that he depended on me. I carried on, because I *had* to carry on, for him."

I'd told myself I felt so alone before, trapped on an island in Puget Sound. But I had to take that all back: I *hadn't* been alone. I'd had someone with me all along, my brother Gilbert, a connection to something outside of myself that existed long before I'd ever come into the astral dimension. Only I hadn't realized it, *wasn't* realizing it, until now, after he was gone.

I looked at Emory. At some point while we were talking, he'd floated closer to me. I don't know if it was something he was doing, or if we'd simply drifted together, but he was less than five feet from me now. Below us, the Earth loomed, solid but separate. Could the shadow creature reach us up here? At that moment, I didn't care.

"Zach," Emory said. "I'm really sorry that he's gone. But for the record, I'm sure they'll find him. Or we will. He'll be back, I promise."

I smiled and realized for the first time that Emory said "for the record" a lot.

I looked back down. At some point as he'd flown up into the heavens, our silver cords had become entwined again, like a braid. This time they were so entangled that I couldn't imagine us ever getting them apart again.

I started to cry. I couldn't help myself, not after everything that happened—the emotion just came bubbling out of me. But it wasn't entirely negative. It was beyond beautiful what I was doing, floating in the space hundreds of miles above the Earth's atmosphere accompanied by my astral boyfriend.

Boyfriend. There was that word again. I'd never even seen Emory in person or touched his physical body. Even so, I already felt so close to him. It was a little like when I'd seen Gilbert for that first time, like he was somehow a part of me, and I was a part of him. He understood what I was feeling—what it felt like to be trapped, vulnerable, how scary it was to have certain things, important things, out of your control. But it was also more than that.

Emory's spirit was closer now, touching me, holding me. It was as if I only existed in the places where we were actually touching, that I was living on the surface of my astral skin. That's when I realized that his real body didn't matter. Emory's gentle astral touch, his tender embrace, was already more intimate than anything we could do with our physical bodies. I reached out and touched his silver cord at last, at the spot where it emerged from the back of his head. It throbbed, warm like mine, yet felt different too, softer, silkier.

Emory was kissing me now, and I was kissing him back. I could taste him—not his physical body, but something else. He tasted clear and clean, like mountain water—pure, but with a definite taste, one that's unique to itself. I thought about how I'd been able to see the shadow creature's thoughts and memories just by touching its eyes. Could I "see" Emory's innermost thoughts now that I was touching his astral body? Somehow I knew I could if I wanted to—his whole being was wide open to me, as mine was to him. But this was something different than what I'd done with the shadow creature. I wasn't touching Emory's mind; I was touching his soul.

That's when the gentle touch, the comfort we were sharing turned to something more, something urgent. It still had something to do with Gilbert, with being consoled by Emory, but now it was more passionate, as if I could somehow lose myself in this soul-kiss, spread what I was feeling out, diffuse it between our souls.

But what I was feeling didn't lessen. Just the opposite happened. Suddenly I was a skyrocket again, finally exploding, but in an explosion that did not end, just grew in an ever-expanding bloom of light and energy. I vaguely remembered how only a few short days ago I had felt so trapped and isolated and alone, living on Hinder Island. Now I felt the opposite of all that, like I was exploding to fill Emory, and he was exploding too—or maybe it was all just one explosion. I still existed only in the point of our kiss, the touch of our embrace, but suddenly that point of impact seemed so much bigger than just the two of us, as if we were expanding to be able touch everything around us—the planet below, the stars above.

Then, without warning, the horizon underneath us began to sizzle in the burst of a sunrise halfway across the world. If this is what it looked like through the smoky lens of the astral dimension, I could only imagine how bright it must've looked unfiltered—literally blinding. A new day was dawning in many more ways than one. And suddenly I was completely consumed by that dazzling light and the warmth of Emory's spirit, and together we were as bright and clean and clear as the universe itself.

17

Later, as we hung entwined in the heavens, I said to Emory, "Well, I guess I know the answer to whether or not we could fly to Jupiter."

He looked up at me. "Hmmm?"

"Remember?" I said. "Before? I wondered if we could visit other planets in the astral dimension?" I nodded toward a bright light out among the stars.

Emory smiled. "Oh, right. But for the record, that's not Jupiter. That's Venus. The brightest natural object in the night sky. A lot of people mix 'em up."

For some reason, this made me think of Gilbert. Once again, I listened for him, but I still couldn't hear anything.

Emory pulled away. "We should get back to Earth."

"People mix up Jupiter and Venus," I said, thinking out loud.

"Sure," Emory said. "It's an easy mistake. They look a lot alike."

"Just like I mixed up Gilbert and Billy."

"What?"

"Before, when we heard Billy crying, and I thought it was Gilbert."

"Oh, right."

I pulled the rest of the way apart from Emory. I felt like an amoeba separating, alone again, though not nearly as cold and alone as before.

"I just got a crazy thought," I said.

"What's that?"

"What if Conrad and Evelyn meant to kidnap Billy, but they got Gilbert instead?"

"Why would they do that?"

"Because Billy's dad told them to."

"Who?" Emory said.

"Billy's father! Billy's parents are divorced, and they're both real jerks. But more than once, I've heard the father saying say how totally unfair it is that the mother got full custody and that she makes him come all the way out to the island to pick Billy up."

I remembered what I'd read about kids who were kidnapped being traded off to someone else—that the person they ended up with wasn't always the person who did the actual kidnapping. I'd thought it had been the woman from the New Age store who had traded Gilbert off to Conrad and Evelyn. But what if it was Conrad and Evelyn who had kidnapped him and were trading him off to Billy's dad? If Billy's dad sent someone who didn't know Billy to kidnap him, it made sense that they might get the wrong kid, especially since the two boys looked so much alike.

The more I thought about this, the more sense it made.

"You're just guessing," Emory said, and he was right. I'd already jumped to the wrong conclusions a couple of times before. "How do we find out for sure?"

I turned myself back toward the Earth. "Well, the first thing I want to do is take another look at Billy."

———

Back on Hinder Island, we flew to the front porch where I'd watched Billy and his mother before.

With their blond hair, Gilbert and Billy really did look alike, especially if you didn't know them.

"Conrad and Evelyn had probably never seen Billy before," I said. "They'd probably just been given a picture. But Billy wasn't in his front yard where his father said he was going to be, and Gilbert was, looking just like him."

"So that's who Conrad and Evelyn are going to meet?" Emory said. "Billy's dad? But he'll know they got the wrong kid. He'll have to let Gilbert go."

I nodded. "That's right! So Gilbert's going to be all right!" I so wanted these words to be true. Why didn't I feel like they were?

Emory looked away.

"What?" I said.

"Nothing," he said quickly. Too quickly.

And that's when I realized what he already knew: if Gilbert recognized Billy's father, the whole plan got exposed. They couldn't just let him go, because Gilbert would know the truth.

"But if they can't send him home," I said, "then they'll have no choice but to…" I couldn't say the words out loud.

If Gilbert recognizes Billy's dad, they'll have no choice but to kill him.

"You need to call the police," Emory said. "You've got a good theory now—probable cause, I bet. They'll listen to you. You've got to go back to your body."

I nodded quickly. "You're absolutely right. I will." But the more I thought about this, the less sense it made.

"What?" Emory said.

"What can the police do? Billy's dad is on the run now. He had to have a plan—if Evelyn and Conrad had taken the right kid, the police would already be on his trail. So they won't know where he is. And there's no time. Conrad and Evelyn went to meet Billy's dad *hours* ago. It might already be too late."

"But you have to try. What choice do we have?"

We can try to find them ourselves from the astral dimension. If nothing else, there was still the needle-in-a-haystack search of the area's airports and marinas.

"You can do both," Emory said. "You can go back to your body and call the police, and *then* come back here and we can see if we can find Billy's dad."

"I've already used my last stick of incense," I said. "Maybe the woman at the New Age store has more, and maybe she'd give them to me. But maybe she won't!" I looked at Emory. "You go. You call the police, tell them what we think, and then come back and meet me."

"And leave you alone here with that creature? The only reason it didn't get you the last time was because I was here to fight it off."

The creature. I'd already forgotten all about it again—had already gotten distracted—even after I'd promised myself I wouldn't. I scanned the shadows around us.

"Zach," Emory said. "We both need to go back. We've already stayed here too long. You know I'm right."

He *was* right, but I didn't answer. Together, we drifted across Billy's front yard in the never-ending astral breeze.

"What can we possibly do?" he went on. "Search the airports? How would we even find the airports from the astral dimension? It's not like we have a map. If it hadn't been for that lighthouse, we might not even have found

Hinder Island in the dark. But there are things the police can do. They can close the airports. They can track Billy's father—maybe find the signal on his cell phone."

I looked over at Emory again. I suddenly had another idea.

"What?" he said.

"I could listen for *him*. For Billy's father."

"But we listened before, for Conrad and Evelyn. We couldn't hear them. What makes you think you'll hear Billy's father?"

Emory had a good point. Then again, I hadn't known Conrad and Evelyn. I didn't really know Billy's father either, but I *had* been listening to him and Billy's mother scream at each other for almost two years now. And I'd been listening in the same dimension that they were in. Maybe that was the key—maybe I hadn't been able to hear Conrad and Evelyn because I'd never heard them in the right dimension.

Either way, I had to try.

Emory was still glancing around the shadows of the front yard—the pools of darkness alongside the abandoned wagon, the swath of blackness under the porch itself. "Whatever we do," he said, "can we at least do it up in the sky?"

I nodded, and we shot up into the open air. Even as we rose, I was already listening for Billy's father, trying to remember exactly what he sounded like.

I was certain it would work. It *had* to.

I didn't hear anything at first, just the same dull, otherworldly roar that I'd been hearing since entering the astral dimension.

"Zach?" Emory said.

I was busy listening for the sound of a man I'd heard many times, but had never really paid any attention to. His arguments with Billy's mom had mostly been an annoyance—noise pollution on an island of peaceful sounds. I'd always tried my best to tune them out.

Still, I'd been able to hear Gilbert that one time. It was a question of focusing, of listening for a specific person, and ignoring all the others.

So I focused.

And suddenly an old man muttered.

Another man laughed.

A third man had called into talk radio and was ranting about immigration politics.

But I knew that none of these was Billy's father.

Emory and I drifted on the ethereal breeze. He stared down at the gathering shadows below us, and I kept listening. As I did, I tried to picture Billy's father. What color was his hair? How old was he? How tall? I wasn't sure—I'd never paid that much attention. Sure, I'd *overheard* him plenty of times, but truthfully, I wasn't sure I'd ever actually spoken to the man. I didn't even know his first name. And yet I thought I could distinguish him from all the other people on the planet?

No! I had to try, to *focus*.

A man gave a scientific lecture of some kind.

Another man tried to sell someone on cabinet refinishing.

Some else sang in the shower.

But I still wasn't hearing Billy's father.

I glanced over at Emory. He looked up at me expectantly.

"Nothing yet," I said.

I tried a different tack. I may not have talked to Billy's father, but I'd talked to Billy plenty of times. And if Billy was his father's biological son, that meant they shared half their genes. That had to count for something, didn't it?

I concentrated on Billy—on the normally happy boy with the sweet laugh.

I immediately heard Billy down on the porch below. The sense of him seemed quite distinctive now—really nothing at all like Gilbert, I realized. Billy was crying again, even louder than before.

I tried blocking the sound and feel of Billy out of my mind while still keeping some sense of him. Then I tried again to tune into his father.

I still didn't hear anything. Emory cleared his throat impatiently.

"I'm trying," I said, a little irritably.

"Just relax," Emory said. "It'll come."

"Well, if you want me to relax, why are you rushing me?"

"Rushing you?" Emory said.

"Forget it," I said, concentrating again.

But right away, Emory cleared his throat again.

"Emory, would you please stop that? It's distracting me."

"Stop what?" he said.

I looked at him, saw the confusion on his face.

"Didn't you just clear your throat?" I said.

"Why would I clear my throat? We're in the astral dimension—no physical body, remember?"

"Oh," I said. "Then…" Who was clearing his throat?

I listened again.

Someone was wheezing. But now when I listened more closely, it was obvious it didn't sound like Emory at all.

Then that same person coughed.

I looked up at Emory. He wasn't coughing or wheezing.

"Zach?" he said. "What's going on?"

I didn't answer, just hovered there, slowly drifting, listening some more. I could now clearly hear the ragged breathing of a heavy smoker. The wheezing sounded like it was coming from right next to me—which is why I'd thought it was Emory. But it wasn't.

I grinned at Emory. "Got him!"

18

We had to fly a long way—miles and miles from Hinder Island, much farther south than the cabin by the lake where we'd first found Gilbert.

But this time I wasn't fumbling along, trying to retrace some forgotten route from earlier. This time I was back to being guided by the sound of a person, which meant we could soar across the sky. Even I felt like Superman now, invulnerable and throbbing with power.

Somehow I knew just when to stop.

"We're here," I said, suspended in the darkness.

We were way beyond even the most rustic of country houses now. It should have been just an ocean of darkness.

And it *was* mostly dark, except for a collection of other worldly lights. They were enormous, five feet across at least, and swaying slightly, like buoys gently rocking in a sea of thick night fog. Even stranger, each light was a slightly different color—muted shades of white, grey, red, yellow, green, blue, and orange.

Meanwhile, strange noises also rose up from below. One sounded like the gurgle of a river, another like pancakes sizzling, one like the hissing of a freeway, and still another sort of like bubbles popping.

What was this, some kind of circus funhouse? But not surprisingly, it was all definitely coming from within the astral realm.

Nothing about this dimension surprised me anymore. Still, I had to know if all this had anything to do with Billy's father.

I knew for a fact that he was down there. I could hear him breathing.

———

It wasn't a funhouse—it was a graveyard. That's where Emory and I found ourselves.

It was an *old* graveyard, maybe even an abandoned one, given the odd angles of some of the gravestones and small monuments jutting up from the uneven ground. In the real world, there was probably nothing much unusual about the place, except maybe its remote location and its age.

But in the astral dimension? I now had a clearer look at the colored lights that I'd seen from above. They were vortexes—like the one Emory and I had seen before back on Hinder Island, the one that had sucked down the spirit of that old man. There were nine in all, each one a different color and each one slowly sucking in on itself like a miniature galaxy. It was their movements that made them look, from above, like they were swaying.

They were also the source of the strange sounds—the popping, the sizzling, the gurgling, and all the rest.

"More inter-dimensional gates," Emory said. "What do you think? Each to a different dimension?"

This made sense. "But whose—" I began.

Emory pointed into the shadows among the gravestones, to something I hadn't noticed at first.

Strange figures stood listlessly among the graves. They were in the astral dimension along with Emory and me, not in the real world. They glowed too, like Emory and me, but dimmer. And they didn't have silver cords.

"Ghosts," Emory said. "Well, I guess that makes sense since this is a graveyard."

"Maybe they're like Alistair," I said. "Somehow they've learned to avoid going through their gates."

"I don't think so," Emory said. "Look at their faces."

There were nine ghosts in all, the same as the number of vortexes. I saw an old woman in a ball gown, a hunched old man in an ill-fitting suit, even a small girl with a bow in her hair. They all wafted slowly around the graveyard. Did the different gates mean that every person went to a different dimension after they died? That was interesting.

Emory was right that there was something wrong with their faces. Their bodies were dimmer than ours, but more or less focused. But their faces were somehow indistinct, blurred and wavering. I couldn't make out their expressions, or even their features. It was the strangest thing. It was like the astral breeze was blowing their faces into some kind of flicking smear even as it left their bodies undisturbed. And since they didn't have eyes, I guess it made sense that they couldn't see us—none of the ghosts seemed to notice Emory's and my arrival.

"Lost souls?" I said. "But why haven't they been sucked into their next dimensions? That's what happened to the man at the other gate."

"Unfinished business?" Emory said. "Or maybe the gates are confused because there's something wrong with their minds. So they're stuck in some sort of limbo."

Emory's theory made as much sense as anything. The gates themselves weren't shifting locations, so maybe they were somehow anchored near the physical bodies of the dead, while their spirits were drawn to the general area, not able to move away, but not willing to move on to the next life either.

Emory floated to the closest of the ghosts, an impossibly skinny old woman simply wrapped in a sheet. "Hello?" he said.

The ghost didn't answer, didn't even turn Emory's direction. If anything, her face got blurrier.

"Forget the ghosts," I said, remembering why we'd come. It had been so easy to be distracted by the figures and rotating vortexes that mesmerized like optical illusions. "We need to find Billy's father."

"Let's just stay away from the gates," Emory said. "They may not detect the ghosts, but I bet they can detect us."

"Where *is* he?" I said, meaning Billy's father. He was the reason we'd come, but I didn't see him anywhere.

"That must be his," Emory said, pointing to a single car parked in the graveyard's gravel parking lot. "Why don't you listen again?"

Duh. I listened again, and immediately sensed him in a patch of gravestones not twenty feet away. A single ember burned orange in the dark—a cigarette. The light from the inter-dimensional gates and the ghosts didn't shine into the material plane, so I hadn't noticed him in the night.

I rocketed closer to him.

Billy's father looked dark and solid—a sharp contrast to the ashen spirits that surrounded us. Still, like those ghosts, it was hard to make out his face. He definitely *had* a face—it was just hidden by the gloom of the graveyard and the dark filter of the astral dimension. All I knew for sure was that he looked more haggard than when I'd seen him last.

I looked around. I didn't see Gilbert anywhere.

"Where is he?" I said to Billy's dad. "Where's my little brother?"

He didn't answer, just took another drag off his cigarette. He thought he was alone in this graveyard.

I stared him in the eye. "*Answer me!*"

Billy's father cleared his throat, still raw. He wasn't hearing me. Nearby, a grey vortex fizzed like churning acid.

"Conrad and Evelyn must not have arrived yet," Emory said, floating behind me. "This must be their meeting place—the place they talked about on the phone. Assuming you're right that he really is the kidnapper."

"I have to be," I said. "Why else would he be in a graveyard in the middle of the night?"

"Then the fact that Gilbert's not here yet is a good thing. Billy's dad doesn't know yet that they've got the wrong kid." He thought for a second. "That means we can go to the police now. If they get here before Conrad and Evelyn, Gilbert will be safe."

Emory was right. We'd made it here in time. I let my anger at Billy's father drain from me like water down a hole in the sand.

"But where are we?" I said. "We don't even know where to tell the police to go."

"A sign," Emory said, already moving toward the parking lot. "We need a street sign or a cemetery sign. Something we can use to identify this place."

Emory was bringing me back to reality. Figuring out where we were and getting word to the police was far more important than having an astral stare-down with Billy's dad.

I followed Emory to the parking lot, but even as we searched for something to identify the location, I remembered again how I didn't even know if Gilbert was still alive.

"He's alive," Emory said out of the blue, as if reading my mind. "Conrad and Evelyn have no reason to kill him. They have no way of knowing they got the wrong kid."

"Then why couldn't I *hear* him?" I said. I admit I was letting despair get the best of me.

"Got it," Emory said.

"What?" I said, confused.

He gestured to a weather-beaten wooden sign between the cemetery and the parking lot.

Durston Memorial Park, it read in faint letters. The name of the cemetery. We could just make it out in the moonlight.

"Now," he said, "let's get back to our bodies, so you can call the police."

But even as he said this, a pair of headlights cut their way into the graveyard gloom.

19

"It's too late!" I said to Emory. "Conrad and Evelyn are here!"

"Maybe it's not them," Emory said, but the car was already turning into the cemetery parking lot. It was a white SUV just like the one we'd seen out at the cabin on Silver Lake.

"Go!" I said to Emory. "*You* go call the police. I'll stay here."

"Zach!"

"Emory, don't argue with me! I'm staying here, but someone needs to call the police. This is the only way."

"But what can you even do from the astral dimension?"

"I don't know. But I'll think of something. Just go!"

Emory stared at me an instant longer. Then I saw the glint in his eyes as he decided I was right, that one of us really did need to call the police. He glanced around the cemetery, trying to make sure that the shadow creature hadn't suddenly reappeared. When he still didn't sense its presence, he looked back me.

"For the record," he said, "I think I love you."

Before I could answer, he relaxed. His astral body was instantly whipped out of sight, back to his physical body. From there, he could call the police and report what he'd seen. But given how far out in the middle of nowhere we were, I had no idea how long it would take them to get here.

Meanwhile, I was left alone with the graveyard's collection of lost, lingering souls. The vehicle was parking, tires crunching on gravel, wan headlights barely slicing through the astral murk. Billy's father was silently working his way through the graves toward the parking lot.

I flew to the SUV ahead of Billy's father. I may have been floating weightless in the astral dimension, but I'd never felt so heavy in my life. There didn't seem to be anything I could *do*. From somewhere back in the graveyard, a green vortex gasped like a drowning man.

In the parking lot, the car doors opened, squeaking like animals in the night. I noticed for the first time that the back windows of the SUV were tinted.

Conrad climbed out one side, and Evelyn huffed her way out of the other.

I'd been right. It really had been Billy's father who was behind Gilbert's kidnapping.

"He'd better be here," Evelyn muttered to Conrad.

"Oh, I'm here," Billy's father said from shadows of the graveyard. Evelyn jerked in surprise. "Where's the boy?"

Conrad faced off with him. "First things first. Where's the money?"

"How is he?" Billy's father said. "Is he scared?"

"I told you on the phone," Conrad said. "Everything's fine. Now where's the money?"

"To hell with the money—let me have my son!" Billy's father stepped closer to the side of the vehicle, tried to open the back door, but found that it was locked.

"He's *fine*," Conrad repeated. "He's sleeping." Evelyn hung back, watching the interaction between the two men.

Gilbert is sleeping? Maybe this was why I'd suddenly been unable to hear him. Maybe something about being asleep made his mind blend, undetectable, into the astral dimension.

I flung myself up over the vehicle, then dipped down through the roof like a speed skater taking a hairpin turn. I stopped myself perfectly in mid-air.

I stared into the dark shadows in the back of the SUV, desperate for any sign of my brother.

The dome light shone on a bit of rumbled clothing. Gilbert. I could see the lump of his body rising and falling as he breathed.

He's okay! He was just sleeping. Relief swept through me like an avalanche.

"Now," Conrad was saying to Billy's father, "about that money."

"You'll get your damn money!" Billy's father said. "I just want to see if he's okay."

Billy's father opened the front door, the side where Evelyn had been sitting.

"No!" I said. "Wait!"

But Billy's father, unable to hear me from the astral dimension, ignored me and reached in to unlock the back door. Then he opened it.

Seeing the blond boy in the backseat, Billy's father sighed, reassured. Everything might still be okay, I realized, just as long as Gilbert didn't wake up. After all, as long as he didn't recognize Billy's father, there was no way for the police to connect any of them to the kidnapping. So what if Gilbert had been out to their lake cabin? It had been late at night. He probably hadn't seen any of the surrounding area—he'd been tied up in the back seat of an SUV. So once Billy's father realized their mistake, he could still have Conrad and Evelyn drop Gilbert off somewhere where someone would find him. No one would be any wiser.

But for that to happen, Billy's father had to realize that Gilbert was not his son. For the time being, he'd mistaken him for Billy just like everyone else.

"It's not your son, you idiot!" I shouted at Billy's father. "They kidnapped the wrong kid!"

"I'll get your money," Billy's father said to Conrad, still not hearing me. Billy's father turned for the graveyard where he must've had the money hidden.

I floated after him, shouting in his ear. "It's not your son!"

"I have to say," Billy's father said back at Conrad, "it's not every stockbroker who performs such personal services." Out among the gravestones again, Billy's father reached behind one of the markers and lifted up a paper grocery bag folded over into a something like a satchel.

Conrad rolled his eyes. "Well, Simon, you didn't give me much choice, now, did you?"

Billy's father—Simon—laughed cruelly. "Should've thought of that before that creative accounting of yours."

This explained how such unlikely kidnappers as Conrad and Evelyn had tried to kidnap Billy in the first place; Simon must have caught them stealing from him. But even that hadn't been enough to convince them. He'd still had to sweeten the deal with cash.

"Just give us the money!" Evelyn said to Simon.

"*It's not your damn son!*" I shouted at Simon one more time, but got no more of a reaction than before.

Conrad met him as he returned to the parking lot, taking the grocery bag from his hand.

"Thanks," Simon said. "For what it's worth."

Evelyn lunged out from behind the SUV, snatching the bag from Conrad. Then she opened it up, trying to count it in the dark. "It's worth a lot more than *this*," she muttered.

"Evelyn," Conrad said, "shut up."

"I hope you're not offended," Simon said, "when I don't recommend you to my friends."

"We're even now," Conrad said. "I won't be offended if I never see you again."

Only now that the money had actually changed hands did Simon finally go to the backseat of the vehicle and start to lift Gilbert out. And only now did he realize that Conrad and Evelyn hadn't quite delivered their share of the bargain.

"What? This isn't my son!"

But everything could still be okay, I knew, just as long as Gilbert didn't wake up.

"Don't wake up," I said to my sleeping brother. "Don't wake up!"

"What are you—" Conrad began.

"*This isn't my son!*" Simon said. "You *idiots!* This is the neighbor kid!"

They'd recognized their mistake, but Gilbert still hadn't woken up. Even now, if Conrad and Evelyn left with Gilbert before he recognized Billy's father, everything could still be okay.

"That's impossible," Evelyn was saying. "You gave us a description. You gave us a photo."

"I know my own damn son!" Simon said. "You morons! How could you get the wrong kid?"

Simon turned and dumped Gilbert, still asleep, back into the backseat.

"Stop!" Evelyn shrieked. "Don't put him back there!"

"What the hell am I supposed to do with him? That's not my son. You need to take him back."

Yes! I thought. *Take him back.*

Evelyn laughed out loud. "Are you out of your mind? We're not taking anyone *back*."

But before she could react, Simon snatched the grocery bag back from her hand.

"Give me that!" she screamed, even louder than before.

"I'm not paying for this," Simon said. "You didn't do your end of the bargain. You got the wrong kid."

"Give her the money," Conrad said, surprisingly calm. When I looked over at him, I saw that Conrad had pulled a gun, and was aiming it right at Simon.

Simon could not have been more unimpressed. "Did you even hear what I said? *You got the wrong damn kid.*"

"Well, that's your problem now. Give her the money." Conrad underlined his words with the barrel of the gun.

Simon shook his head in disgust. "I can't believe you got the wrong kid. You're an even worse kidnapper than you are a stockbroker."

Suddenly from the back of the SUV, Gilbert moaned. Simon, Conrad, and Evelyn all fell silent, then turned and looked over at the vehicle.

Floating weightless in the astral dimension, I moaned too. "No! Don't wake up, Gilbert. Go back to sleep."

In the backseat of the SUV, Gilbert squirmed upright.

"Don't do this!" I shouted at my little brother. "Go back to sleep! You hear me? Go back to sleep."

But Gilbert didn't hear. The door to the SUV was still open, and Simon was standing just outside. And even in the dim glow of the vehicle's dome light, Gilbert spotted him right away, someone he knew.

"Mr. Scanlon?" Gilbert said. "Is that you?" Despite the bindings on his feet and hands, he crawled out of the backseat and stumbled over to Simon, immediately trying to wrap himself around Simon's legs. "Mr. Scanlon, help me! They took me away."

So that was it. Gilbert had recognized him.

Simon looked up at Conrad and Evelyn in disgust. "You idiots." Then he pulled a gun of his own out of his pants.

"What are you doing?" Conrad said nervously.

"What do you think I'm doing? He recognizes me. How the hell am I supposed to explain that?"

And here we were, exactly where I'd feared we'd be all along: Billy's father was going to kill Gilbert. From behind me in the cemetery, the gurgling vortex seemed almost to burp.

I had to *do* something. But what could I possibly do from the astral dimension?

Even Conrad was shocked by what Billy's father had said. He lowered his own gun. "Simon, you're not thinking about—"

"What do you suggest I do? By all rights, I should have you do it, but you'd probably screw this up, too. So I'll have to do it myself. So go on, get out of here, both of you."

Conrad and Evelyn glanced at each other.

"Get in the car," Conrad said to her.

"What about the money?" Evelyn said.

"Forget the damn money," Conrad said. "Just get in the goddamn car!"

Conrad practically leapt into the SUV and twisted the ignition. The engine squealed a little before finally starting. Evelyn hesitated, staring daggers at Simon. But then she turned, huffing for the vehicle. She slammed the back-door closed.

"Wait!" I shouted at them. "You can't just leave! He's going to kill him. He's just a little boy. You can't let him kill him."

Without another word, Evelyn climbed primly into the front seat. The second she was inside, Conrad threw it into reverse, and the SUV scraped its way backward on the gravel. Once clear, he gave it more gas, and it roared out of the graveyard parking lot.

Gilbert had watched the whole interaction with a confused look on his face. But one thing about this whole experience seemed to make sense, and that was the fact that Mr. Scanlon was the father of his best friend, Billy. He seemed to cling to this fact much the way he was still holding onto the man's leg.

"Well," Simon said to Gilbert. "Let's get you untied." He latched the safety on his gun, then tucked the whole thing into his belt. He bent down to undo Gilbert's feet.

"Mr. Scanlon?" Gilbert said. "Why do you have a gun?"

"It's all right, Gilbert," Simon said calmly. "It's just a toy."

He was really going to kill him.

I had to do *something*.

It had seemed like Evelyn had started to hear me shouting at her from the astral dimension, out at the cabin on Silver Lake. And I'd definitely felt whatever evil astral being had touched me that afternoon out at Trumble Point. It *was* possible to communicate between the astral realm and the material one. Somehow I was going to get through to Simon now. I had to.

"Listen—" I started to say to Simon.

Even as I did, I felt something I hadn't before—a rough yank on the back of my head, like I was a dog and someone had jerked hard on my leash. If I'd been in the real world in physical form, a violent wrench like that would have broken my neck for sure.

But I wasn't in the real world—I was in the astral dimension. And I was suddenly being flung away from that graveyard by the back of my head. It felt like my brain was being jerked from my skull.

In terms of pain, it seemed endless, a Big Bang of sensation that exploded outward from my head. But at the same time, I knew it had all happened in a flash, in an instant.

I opened my eyes. The sharp pain was already subsiding, as quickly as it had started. But my head pounded, and my teeth ached. The light was different, much brighter than it had been an instant before—too bright. Something or someone loomed over me.

I was too dazed to make sense of where I was. I knew I was in someplace different than that cemetery in the night. But while my body was here in this new place, it was like my mind, my thoughts, were still back in that other place.

Finally, my thoughts started to catch up with my body.

I was back in my bedroom, back on Hinder Island.

"Zachary?" my grandmother was saying. She was the figure I'd sensed looming over me.

I stared at her, still trying to make sense of what had just happened. Then it hit me like another yank out of the blue: my grandmother had woken me up. My mind and body had been reunited, and my astral projection had come to an end.

20

I looked, blinking, at my grandmother. The light was so bright, so much stronger than it had been just seconds before. Gravity pressed me to the bed like Lilliputian cables.

"What did you *do*?" I said to my grandmother. I couldn't have hidden the outrage in my voice even if I wanted to. Simon had been about to shoot Gilbert in that cemetery—I needed to get back!

"Do?" my grandmother said, taken aback. "I woke you up. You were having a nightmare."

"It wasn't a dream! It was real!"

My grandma stared at me like I was crazy. But if I told her the truth, she'd think I *was* crazy.

I took a breath. "I'm sorry, Grandma. You just surprised me. But I have to go back to bed. Okay? Do you mind? I have to go back to bed *right now.*"

That's when I remembered I didn't have any more incense. I couldn't go back to the astral dimension even if I wanted to. Realizing this was like running into a brick wall at full speed.

My grandma ignored me. "I wanted to tell you the good news."

The words cut like a horn through the fog of my brain. "Good news?" My grandma didn't look like a mummy anymore. Now she had the energy of a ballet dancer. I'd never seen her stand so tall.

"There's been a tip," she said. "The police got a report of someone matching Gilbert's description near some old cemetery. They think it might be the kidnappers!"

Emory got through to the police.

"But apparently it's out in the middle of nowhere," my grandmother went on, "so it could be hours before we hear anything."

Hours? Gilbert didn't have hours. He didn't even have minutes!

I needed to get back there. But I wasn't sure that was even possible without the special incense.

"I'm sorry, Grandma," I said. "I feel terrible. Do you mind? I need to go back to bed." I was trying to be convincing, but

I wasn't doing it very well, was definitely acting strange. We finally hear news about Gilbert, and I want to go back to bed?

But the fact was things *were* strange. Gilbert had been kidnapped. Besides, my grandma was plenty distracted herself.

So she said, "I'll wake you if we hear anything else." Then she was gone.

I wanted to bolt the door to make sure she didn't interrupt me again, but there was no lock—they'd never let me get one for fear of what I might do on the Internet. I just had to hope that my grandparents didn't come back.

I turned to the incense holder on my nightstand. The incense was gone, burned completely down to the nub.

I picked up the ashes, grey and fine, and crumbled them under my nose. I couldn't smell any trace of what I'd smelled before, that scent of decomposing forest.

So I had to do it without the incense. Emory had done it.

He'd also said it had taken him his whole life, plus years of intense meditation, to figure out how.

But I'd been to the astral dimension before. I already knew what it felt to separate your spirit from your body. That had to count for something.

So I lay back in bed and tried to remember how to do the astral projection thing. Celestia Moonglow had said something about deep breaths and imagining a point of light.

I breathed deeply, in and out. I tried to imagine the stress blowing from my body.

There isn't time for this, I thought. *Gilbert is in danger!* My head hurt.

I tried again. I imagined the point of light resting on my throbbing forehead. I imagined it rising up above my head. I imagined my spirit floating free, joining that point.

But it *was* all in my imagination. I was still pinned to the bed. It wasn't working.

And it wasn't *going* to work. There was no way I was going to be able to *relax* knowing that Gilbert could be dead at any second.

I couldn't let that happen.

This time, I let myself get angry, let the fury rise like bile in my throat. I focused on the throbbing pain behind my eyes, let it swell to consume my whole head. I would tear my spirit from my body if I had to!

I strained. I writhed inside myself. I tried to *rip* my spirit right out of my physical body.

And then suddenly my spirit sat upright in bed.

———

How long had it taken me to talk to my grandmother, then force myself back into the astral dimension? Two minutes? Three? I didn't know, and I also didn't know how long it would take me to get back to Gilbert.

I listened for my brother.

I immediately heard him breathing—I could hear him loud and clear. He was still alive. I didn't know for how much longer, but at least it wasn't too late yet.

I didn't have time to fly all the way back to the grave-yard, even in the soaring, friction-less way I'd managed before. No, I needed to be there ten minutes ago. How did I get back when it was so far away?

Except the astral realm wasn't a physical dimension—even *Voyage Beyond the Rainbow* had said that. And if it wasn't a physical dimension, he wasn't really far away. I'd been able to hear things even across a great distance, so maybe it was possible to somehow travel those distances in an instant, too.

I closed my eyes and focused on the sound of my brother's breathing.

I concentrated on that breathing, let it grow in my mind. It was there, and I was here, but all that stood between us was distance, a mere gap in space—a space that supposedly didn't even exist in the astral dimension. At the same time, I fanned the flicking flames of the anger that had let me reenter the astral dimension in the first place.

Then I let that anger explode again. I let myself go. Suddenly I was a gunshot and Gilbert's breathing was the bull's-eye.

When I opened my eyes again, I found myself waver-ing unsteadily at the edge of the gravel parking lot at Dur-ston Memorial Park.

I'd done it.

But the fog was not yet gone from my mind. It took me a moment to make sense of my darkened surroundings.

To one side, over in the graveyard, the rotating vortexes twisted around like so many otherworldly windmills. On the other side of me, a faceless ghost in a frayed pinafore danced a lazy two-step.

Conrad and Evelyn's SUV was long gone. The only car left was Simon's. Directly in front of me he and Gilbert were walking hand in hand into the graveyard. Simon had removed the bounds around my little brother's feet and hands.

"Where are we going?" Gilbert asked Simon.

"Just for a little walk," the man said. "Then I'll take you right home to your parents. You've been away a long time, haven't you?"

I remembered the gun in Simon's belt.

I'd been so eager to get back here, but I was in the astral dimension with no way to contact the real world.

Simon was taking Gilbert into the graveyard to shoot him, and there still wasn't anything I could do about it.

21
—

I flew to my little brother's side.

"Gilbert!" I said into his ear. "Listen to me—it's your brother, Zach. You've got to run from Mr. Scanlon. He's trying to hurt you. Run!" I'd been able to force my spirit into the astral dimension and across a great distance through sheer willpower, so it made sense to me that I could make myself heard in the real world though willpower too.

But Gilbert didn't react.

"I don't wanna go for a walk," Gilbert said to Simon. "I wanna go home."

"Soon," Simon said. "Very soon."

"Gilbert!" I shouted. "Please! I'm right next to you. Run! I'm telling you to run—run as fast as you can!"

Fifteen feet or so into the graveyard, Simon released Gilbert's hand. "Here we go," he said.

"What?" Gilbert said.

"Look over there," Simon said, pointing off into the darkness.

"It's too dark," Gilbert said. "I don't see anything."

As my brother squinted into the night, Simon took a step backward, behind him. As he did, he slipped the gun from his belt and unlatched the safety. He was going to shoot Gilbert in the back of his head. Nearby, a vortex groaned.

"Run, Gilbert! *Please* run!" I was still shouting at my little brother, but it wasn't making any difference.

Suddenly a set of headlights winked into view on the horizon. It had to be the police.

Simon jerked toward the lights, stiffening.

But as quickly as the headlights had appeared, they began to glide away. It hadn't been the police, or even a car on its way to the graveyard—just some lonely vehicle on its way down some forgotten country road. Still, Simon had to know he couldn't shoot Gilbert just yet. Someone in that car might hear.

So with Simon momentarily distracted, I fell down right in front of Gilbert. "Now's your chance!" I said. "Run! Run away!"

This time, Gilbert tilted his head in my direction, as if he actually heard some vague whisper.

I kept at it. "Run, Gilbert, please, run! Run and hide! This is your brother talking! Do it now!"

Gilbert looked back toward the parking lot, and the road beyond.

"Go!" I went on. "Don't think, just do it! Go! *Now*, you little Nabothian cyst!"

At this, at the sound of my calling him my special nickname for him, something changed on Gilbert's face. Even in the darkened moonlight, I saw a flicker of recognition that quickly melted into something like a decision.

He broke for the parking lot.

"That's it!" I called after him. "Go! Run for your life!"

Simon immediately sensed the boy's flight. He turned after him. "Gilbert? Where are you going?"

I stepped in front of him. "Leave him alone, you bastard! He's just a little boy!"

Simon walked right through me, the same way Evelyn had in the cabin at Silver Lake. But what I felt was different than when she'd done it, that little spiderweb-like brush. Now it was like swimming in a warm ocean, and you suddenly pass through a pocket of icy water. It wasn't as cold as the chill of the shadow creature, but it was still unnerving.

"Gilbert?" he called. "Don't run away. Don't you want me to take you home?"

In my astral form, I zoomed after Gilbert.

"Don't listen to him!" I shouted. "Keep running!"

I beat Simon to the parking lot. There I saw that Gilbert had ducked down behind the old weather-beaten sign, the one Emory had found that had the name of the cemetery. Gilbert had run, yes, but only as far as the parking lot. And he'd hidden, but in the most obvious hiding place of all. What did I expect? He was only seven years old. Nearby an old ghost in a hospital gown stared past me, her face as vacant as an empty grave.

Simon would find him hiding there for sure. Gilbert had to keep running. But to where? There were no houses in sight, but the main road wasn't too far off. There weren't very many cars this late at night, but it was still his best chance for help.

"Run for the road!" I said to Gilbert. "Do it now, you little Nabothian cyst!"

Simon stepped around the sign. "Gilbert?" he said gently. "What are you doing? Don't you want me to take you home?"

It was too late. Simon had found him again. Staring up at him with eyes as large as two moons, Gilbert whimpered softly.

I stared at Gilbert, feeling completely powerless to help.

And that's when the shadow creature attacked me again.

22

It came at me from behind. The tentacle-like legs of the shadow creature clamped down around my head. I'd been so distracted by what was going on with Gilbert that it had caught me totally by surprise. In spite of Emory's warnings, I'd forgotten all about it.

This time it didn't completely cover my face. This time I could see it, could watch what was happening to me.

It was even blacker than I remembered, so much it almost hurt to look at it. But within all that darkness, I saw its eyes staring down at me—those horrible, white human eyes, greedy, but intensely intelligent. What were they doing on the *underside* of the creature? Now I knew for a fact they could move.

At the same time, a projection, like the stinger of a mosquito, emerged from underneath those eyes. It stretched out and around, aiming for my forehead.

The creature jammed the stinger down right into my astral skull. I expected to hear it—for it to make sucking or a gurgling sound—but it didn't. It punctured my brain in complete silence.

I understood exactly what was happening. The point of contact was the flip side of the soul-kiss I'd shared with Emory up in the heavens. Rather than trying to join spirits with me or make me feel one with the universe, the creature was attempting to overpower me, to eliminate me, to subtract me from the world.

On some level, I was repulsed by what was happening, the fact that this alien thing was trying to violate my mind.

But I didn't feel any pain. On the contrary, everything I had been feeling—my desperate need to help Gilbert, the frustration of not being able to *do* anything, even the throb in my head—suddenly disappeared, replaced by an almost soothing numbness. It was as if the creature's stinger was releasing some kind of spiritual anesthetic, like what a mosquito injects to mask the pain of its sting. It must have done the same thing when it had attacked me before.

On one hand, I knew I wanted this horrible thing off of me, far away from me.

On the other hand, it was almost nice to finally feel relief from the all the pain and frustration.

I didn't want Gilbert to die, but I finally realized that it was all out of my control anyway—that it had *always* been out of my control.

The creature began to change, to silently metamorphose into something even less substantial, like heavy smoke, like the strange incense that had brought me to the astral dimension in the first place. It was as if the body of the creature was beginning to seep, eyes and all, down through the stinger directly into the center of my astral brain.

I watched it, transfixed, amused. I took back what I said about being disgusted by it—I wasn't now. The creature had been right to attack me. I was weak. I wasn't strong enough to fight the shadow creature off alone. But Emory was gone now, so there wasn't any point in fighting back at all. I shouldn't have come to the astral dimension in the first place, and after I did, I should've listened when Emory said it was time to go home again. I hadn't, and now I was paying the price. I deserved this.

The creature entered me, silently slithered its way into my soul. I could feel it slowly filling me, could feel it on the inside, in places I'd never felt anything before, in places that I didn't think had any feeling. I didn't want the creature to possess my soul and return to the world of humans, as it had done so many times before. I knew for a fact just how much evil this being had done, and could do again. But there was nothing I could do.

It didn't feel bad. I didn't feel anything, but that lack of feeling was almost a relief. What would it mean, being possessed by the creature? Would I simply cease to exist? Maybe I'd be placed safely away in some restful little corner of my mind, a peaceful island oasis, an island in my own mind.

An island. That's where I belonged, somewhere safe and protected and predictable. That's where I'd *always* belonged. I'd been wrong to ever think I could leave. I'd come home—my *real* home. I could finally relax at last.

But in the silence of the creature's invasion of my soul, I suddenly heard a sound. It was quiet, like it was coming from far, far away, but somehow it penetrated even deeper into my soul than the creature's stinger.

It was the release of the safety on a gun.

Gun? I thought.

A smoker wheezed.

Then I remembered Simon, who had no idea what was happening between the shadow creature and me, was still trying to kill Gilbert.

Gilbert.

My little brother, the one person I'd had a connection with all along, even if I hadn't realized it.

If I gave up, if I gave into the creature and leaned back into a lazy hammock on that island in my mind, Gilbert was going to die. In order to save him, I couldn't give into the creature—I had to somehow fight back.

I turned toward my brother. Through the clutch of the shadowy creature, I saw him lying on the ground in front of me. He was bawling his head off. I wasn't sure how I hadn't heard the sound of his crying before, had only heard the click of the safety.

Simon stood in front of Gilbert pointing the gun at him.

"No," I whispered, to both Simon and to the creature on the top of my head—and now inside me as well.

The creature tightened its grip on me, like a python being threatened by the loss of its prey.

"No!" I said again, louder. This time, it was directed entirely at the creature. I reached up and touched it, the shadow of a spider-octopus that had attached itself to my head. It felt more pliable and much slicker than before, a greasy, deflated beach ball underneath a haze of smoke. But at least there was still something there for me to touch. It wasn't too late.

Once again, I seemed to have caught the creature by surprise. It no doubt remembered the last time it had attacked me, how I had accidentally brushed its mind, but also how it had overpowered me anyway, how it would have possessed me if Emory hadn't helped me at the last second. Still, I was alone this time, and the creature probably hadn't considered that I might fight back this far into its metamorphosis, especially after anesthetizing me with its stinger.

It had misjudged me. I wasn't as weak as it thought, and I was tired of living on islands.

Slowly, finger by greasy finger, I pried the thing off my face. It writhed, undulating like an eel on a hook. It made noise now, squealing with outrage. But I kept pulling it off me, felt it slipping, inch by inch, out of my soul. It had to know it was losing this battle.

The stinger was the last thing to leave my head. I felt nothing when it popped free, no pain, no physical sensation at all. But the second it was gone, I felt a brewing of all the emotions it had silenced—the isolation, the frustration, but also the determination and sense of self.

Most of all, I felt anger. I didn't try to suppress it, to get in its way. That anger had worked for me twice before, by getting me back to the graveyard and by helping me communicate with Gilbert. It wasn't the clarity of mind that Celestia Moonglow had talked about, or that I'd felt when I'd first arrived in the astral dimension. But in a way, I finally had my focus back.

With all my might, I threw the creature to one side. It squealed once more, then pulsated away—but awkwardly, flapping like a jellyfish, not surging like a octopus. Like it was injured somehow.

I ignored it and turned toward Simon. This time he wasn't bothering to take Gilbert into the cemetery. This time he was going to take care of things right in the parking lot.

He raised his gun and pointed it right at Gilbert's head.

23

With a scream of outrage, I flew right at Simon.

As before, my astral body passed right through his physical one.

But this time, I took Simon's spirit with me. Simon's physical body fell completely limp, and his spectral body floated free. His spirit even had a silver cord billowing out of the back of his head, like plasma fuel from a leaking spaceship.

I hadn't planned this or thought about it at all. But it made sense in retrospect. After all, I knew that spirits had some sort of a physical form in the astral dimension—Emory's and mine did anyway. Spirits had some sort of physical aspect even when they were still attached to bodies. When I'd passed through Evelyn's and Simon's bodies, I'd definitely felt *something*. And whatever I'd felt that afternoon out at Trumble Point, it had touched something in me.

Mostly, though, I think it happened because I so desperately wanted it to. I was learning that a surprising number of impossible things were possible if you just wanted them badly enough.

Simon's spirit body floated upright, unsteady in the astral dimension. "Huh?" he said, confused, already slipping on the greased surface of the astral dimension. "Where the hell am I?" Finally his eyes focused on me. "Where did *you* come from?" He didn't even realize what had happened—that he was no longer a physical being.

"Leave my little brother alone!" I said, facing off against him like a sumo wrestler.

Simon glanced down at his hand. But he carried no gun with him into the astral dimension. He grimaced, confused and frightened.

Then the shadow creature pounced on him from behind, like a cat on a wounded mouse. It had already somehow collected itself and gathered its strength. It quickly scurried right up to his head and latched itself over Simon's face.

"Wh—"

I held back, surprised by this development.

Simon was too disoriented to put up a fight against the creature. Effortlessly it slid its stinger into Simon's forehead and quickly began flowing down into his brain. The shell of Simon somehow seemed to be a perfect fit for the creature, welcoming and hospitable.

It was right then that Emory swooped down next to me. He'd returned to the astral dimension.

"Are you okay?" he asked.

I nodded even as I kept staring at what was happening to Simon. Emory didn't say a word, just watched the ongoing transformation with me. I knew he'd figure out what was happening fast enough.

"We need to help him," Emory said, immediately floating forward.

I held out a hand to stop him. "No. Wait." It was horrible what was happening, but some part of me told me to let it happen. Was it the petty, vengeful part of me?

In seconds, the shadow creature was gone. Simon had been completely unprepared for the attack so it had poured right down into his soul—or maybe he'd just been even weaker than me.

But the creature hadn't disappeared completely. Two very familiar eyes peered out at me, just as greedy, just as horrible when peering out from a human face. Simon's feeble soul had been conquered, pushed aside into his own dank little island in his mind. The shadow creature, meanwhile, had found a fresh new host.

Simon's astral form, now totally in the creature's control, smiled at me with the self-satisfied grin of a snake. He began to speak, but not in Simon's voice. It was an unsettling rasp.

"Ahhhhh," it said. "This soul will do just fine."

With that, he began to relax, and Simon's silver cord buckled, preparing to pull his now-possessed spiritual body back to his physical body.

At first I thought I'd made a mistake, that my desire for revenge meant something really bad was about to happen.

Then I had an idea.

I shot forward, my arms stretched out in front of me. I grabbed Simon's astral projection around the waist. Then with all the mental strength I could muster, I carried us all toward the closest vortex, a dark one slowly spinning at the edge of the parking lot.

Simon's astral projection squealed, not like the man he had once been, but like the shadow creature he had become. I was too late: I slammed the shadow-possessed Simon directly into the center of the slow-motion cyclone. The creature was too surprised to struggle, to even fight back. It had all happened too fast.

Simon was immediately sucked away, like human waste down a vacuum toilet.

I rolled to one side, desperate to avoid the suction of the vortex. But it turned out to be unnecessary. With Simon sucked into its gullet, the vortex quickly whirled in on itself, disappearing without a trace. Since no part of me had been inside the gate, it hadn't tried to take me with it. Meanwhile, the silver cord that had connected Simon's soul to his body was cut in half, and now it was winding through the air, slowly fading like the moon at dawn.

I immediately turned to my little brother, still stretched out, crying, on the gravel.

"Gilbert!" I said, crouching near him, trying to caress him in a spectral hug. "Are you all right? Everything's okay. I'll be right here until help comes."

Gilbert's tears began slow. He sat upright.

Emory levitated next to me. "He'll be fine now," he said. Sure enough, as if specifically to reassure me, the faint sound of sirens rose in the distance.

That's when I turned to Emory and smiled.

"For the record," I said, "I think I love you, too."

EPILOGUE

Two mornings later, I knocked on my little brother's bedroom door.

"Yeah?" he said from inside.

I entered. "Good morning!" I said.

"Hi." He was still in bed in his pajamas, but it looked like he was wide awake, like he'd been staring out the open window.

"How are you doing?" I asked. "Are you feeling okay?" I'd talked to him the day before when the police had finally brought him home, but it had been in front of my grandparents. He'd gone to bed after that and slept for almost sixteen hours. I hadn't yet had a chance to talk to him alone.

"There's a green ladybug," he said quietly. He wasn't looking out the window after all, but down at the windowsill. "I've never seen a green ladybug. I didn't even know they came green."

"Yeah?" I said. "Me neither."

"It's bad luck to kill a ladybug, but I wonder if that's true of green ladybugs."

"I think it's bad luck to kill most things. Now come on, let's go get some breakfast."

I expected him to say something else about green ladybugs. But instead he said, completely seriously, "You were there."

"What? Where?" I pulled out the chair from his desk and took a seat across from the bed.

"With me," he said. "That night in the cemetery. You were with me."

How could he have known this? Before coming in here, I'd reminded myself not to mention anything about the cabin out on Silver Lake, or even what had happened at the cemetery—stuff that I would've had no way of knowing about if I hadn't been there. Had he sensed me somehow?

I watched him watching the ladybug. "That's impossible," I said. "How could I have been with you?"

"I dunno." His bright eyes met mine at last. "But you were."

I smiled. "Maybe I was." I couldn't lie to him, not after everything that had happened. And when I thought about it, it figured that Gilbert had some idea. After all, he'd heard me. Maybe somehow the whole thing made sense to his seven-year-old mind.

"You think I was going to let anything happen to my brother?" I said. "Never."

There were bad people and bad things in the world. I knew that now. My grandparents had been right about evil—even if they'd also been wrong to think it didn't exist on Hinder Island. It was everywhere, all around us at any moment, maybe even part of us in a way. And that was the kind of thing that, once you knew it, you couldn't ever forget.

But evil wasn't the only force in the world. There was good too, even if it didn't fly around the astral dimension in the form of unicorns and golden dragons, which seemed like it'd only be fair. Even if the only place it existed was inside our hearts.

"You know what?" I went on. "I'm not sure other people would understand what happened that night in the cemetery. So let's not tell Grandpa and Grandma about it, okay?"

Gilbert gently petted the shell of ladybug. "You killed that man."

"Sort of," I said. "I had to make it so he couldn't hurt you."

"How?"

I thought about how I wanted to answer this. "It's complicated. And everything I did was dangerous. I took a shortcut I shouldn't have taken, went somewhere I shouldn't have gone. I wouldn't have done it, except to help you."

"Are you ever going to do it again?"

At that moment, the ladybug fluttered out the window and away.

And I just smiled.

———

The sunlight poured down on me as if from a bucket. Seagulls circled overhead as the ferry approached the mainland dock.

It was a week and a half later, in late July. Emory and I had IM'd and emailed a few times—he'd used the computer at the library—but I hadn't seen him since that night in the cemetery. We were dying to meet again, but we weren't about to go back into the astral realm just yet, so we'd brainstormed this plan for how we might actually get together. He'd told his mom he needed to take some pictures of the Hinder Island ferry terminal for a summer school project. She'd agreed to drive him there and drop him off while she ran some errands. The plan was for us to accidentally meet and become friends, and then later Emory could invite me over to his house for future visits.

The ferry pulled up to the pier. The main road headed from the landing up the hill, then off to the freeway and beyond. Meanwhile, a paved walking trail headed north along the water—all the way to Canada, for all I knew.

But I didn't see Emory.

As the operators tied up the boat, I looked back at Hinder Island. It was closer to the mainland than I remembered, but smaller, too. I could see the whole island from here, an emerald dome against the blue summer sky.

Since I was a foot passenger, I disembarked ahead of the cars. I stepped off the boat onto the dock, then off the dock onto the sidewalk.

Emory was waiting to one side.

I'd expected him to look different, and he did. But it wasn't because of the wheelchair. I'd anticipated that, so it didn't count. No, it was because I was seeing him in the real world, not the astral dimension. So he looked a little darker than I expected, definitely drabber, and maybe a little more frazzled. But at the same time, he looked more focused and more solid, set in place, like the sidewalk that we stood on compared to the rocking ferry behind me.

I stepped closer.

"Hi," I said.

"Hi," he said. There was just no way around this first awkward exchange.

"Wow," I said, gesturing down. "Talk about your phantom limbs."

He rolled his eyes. "That's amputees, you idiot, not paraplegics."

"Hey, give me a break," I said. "I've been working on that line all afternoon."

"I bet you were." But he was smiling when he said this.

I bent down to hug him. His body felt different than it had in the astral dimension—just as solid, but stiffer, and warmer too, toasted by the sun. And he had hard muscles that clenched in his upper body, something I definitely didn't expect, and he had a scent that I wasn't prepared for either—a fresh lemony musk.

Then my arm brushed the skin of his neck, and I instantly felt the same connection I'd felt in the astral dimension, the feeling that the spot where we touched was the only place I existed. It might have been even stronger in the real world than it had been in the astral one.

I gasped, feeling him deep in my soul.

Emory felt it too. His face lit up, even in the bright sun.

I hugged him again, a real hug this time, and kissed him too, suddenly not caring what anyone seeing us might think. Out on the water, the sunlight broke into pieces, a thousand golden needles spread out across the bay.

"You're really real," he whispered into my shoulder. "You're not just a figment of my imagination."

He was crying. I felt like crying, too, but I didn't, and I wondered if this was the way it worked in relationships: taking turns feeling the intense or negative emotions.

I pulled back at last. "How much time do we have?"

"Not long," he said. "The ferry was running late, so we only have thirty minutes or so until my mom gets back. Where should we go?"

"This way," I said, my hand on his shoulder, starting up the trail along the water with him alongside me. "Let's see just how far we can get."

About the Author

Brent Hartinger is the author of a number of novels for teenagers, including *Geography Club* and *The Last Chance Texaco*. His many writing honors include being named the winner of the Scandiuzzi Children's Book Award, a GLAAD Media Award, a Lambda Award, and a Book Sense Pick (four times). In addition to writing novels, he teaches creative writing at Vermont College, founded and edits the fantasy website TheTorchOnline.com, writes for AfterElton.com, and laments the fact that he has virtually no free time. Visit him online at www.brenthartinger.com